John Creasey – Master Story

Born in Surrey, England in 19
there were nine children, John
master story teller and international sensation. Writing under multiple pseudonyms, his more than 600 crime, mystery and thriller titles have now sold 80 million copies in 25 languages. These include many popular series such as *Gideon of Scotland Yard, The Toff, Dr Palfrey* and *The Baron.*

Never one to sit still, Creasey had a strong social conscience, and stood for Parliament several times, along with founding the One Party Alliance which promoted the idea of government by a coalition of the best minds from across the political spectrum..

He also founded the Crime Writers' Association, which to this day celebrates outstanding crime writing. The Mystery Writers of America bestowed upon him the Edgar Award for best novel and then in 1969 the ultimate Grand Master Award. John Creasey's stories are as compelling today as ever.

BY THE SAME AUTHOR
Published or to be published by House of Stratus

GIDEON OF SCOTLAND YARD	(22 TITLES)
THE TOFF	(59 TITLES)
INSPECTOR WEST	(43 TITLES)
THE BARON	(47 TITLES)
DR. PALFREY	(34 TITLES)
DEPARTMENT 'Z'	(28 TITLES)

Go Away To Murder
(Inspector West Leaves Town)

John Creasey

Copyright © 1943 John Creasey Literary Management Ltd

All rights reserved. No part of this publication may be reproduced, stored in a retrieval system, or transmitted, in any form, or by any means (electronic, mechanical, photocopying, recording, or otherwise), without the prior permission of the publisher. Any person who does any unauthorised act in relation to this publication may be liable to criminal prosecution and civil claims for damages.

The right of John Creasey to be identified as the author of this work has been asserted.

This edition published in 2011 by House of Stratus, an imprint of Stratus Books Ltd., Lisandra House, Fore Street, Looe, Cornwall, PL13 1AD, U.K.

www.houseofstratus.com

Typeset, printed and bound by House of Stratus.

A catalogue record for this book is available from the British Library and the Library of Congress.

ISBN 07551 - 2385 - 9
EAN 978 - 07551 - 2385- 8

This book is sold subject to the condition that it shall not be lent, resold, hired out, or otherwise circulated without the publisher's express prior consent in any form of binding, or cover, other than the original as herein published and without a similar condition being imposed on any subsequent purchaser, or bona fide possessor.

This is a fictional work and all characters are drawn from the author's imagination. Any resemblance or similarities to persons either living or dead are entirely coincidental.

Mark Lessing Moves In

A TALL MAN with a roman nose jumped down from the rear of a removal van, and waved to the girl who opened the door of a small modern house in Bell Street, Fulham. After him, two grey-haired men wearing green baize aprons climbed with more circumspection to the roadway as the girl walked to the gate of a small drive. In the shadows of the doorway she had looked attractive: as she came into the bright sunlight of the street the sun shone on her auburn hair, and made her teeth sparkle.

'And you've had no heart attack yet?' she teased.

'You're so heartless you wouldn't know.' The man joined her, while the driver of the van manoeuvred to get the rear of his vehicle square so that he could back up to the front door. Stentorian of voice, the greyheads gave him directions. 'Janet,' continued the roman-nosed man, 'I've been wondering whether you're making a mistake? Giving way to this generous impulse might do a lot of harm. It isn't too late to send the furniture to a warehouse.'

'Don't be a silly ass, Mark. Neither Roger nor I would let you do anything else.'

'I might have to stay for a long time,' Mark warned her. 'Flats are the devil to get.'

'It's the sensible thing to do. I'll show the men the rooms. You look after your precious china.' Janet half-turned, and then said: 'What's the time?'

'Just after two.'

'Roger was going to be in by half-past one.'

Janet hurried to the house, and Mark Lessing stood aside, while the van snarled its way into the drive. Lessing watched intently, but not all his thoughts were on his collection of china and old porcelain in a packing case. He was genuinely doubtful about this move. His landlord had needed his flat for a family emergency, and he had contemplated spending weeks, perhaps months, in a club or a hotel. Then Chief Inspector West of Scotland Yard had told him to stop being an ass, and to occupy the two spare rooms in the Bell Street house. There was room for him, his china, and most of his books. Those were near the back of the van about to be unloaded. The heavier furniture was to be stored until he found a flat in central London at a rent not aimed at millionaires.

His relief at the prospect of keeping his precious porcelain under his own eye was considerable. Janet West had once said that his collection was not only his father and mother, but his wife and children; he was coming to agree with her.

He was anxious to remain within easy distance of Westminster not only because he liked London's West End but because he worked at the Home Office.

He watched Janet, who was giving instructions to the men on the doorstep. Was she really worried because Roger was late?

Mark wondered, as he often did, what it must be like for a man to be loved as Janet loved Roger. And for that matter, to love. Old enough to consider himself a confirmed bachelor, sometimes posing as a misogynist, Mark felt rueful. It seemed only yesterday when he had deplored the fact that Roger was to get married: now he found himself almost envious.

The packing case was carried into one of the downstairs rooms and left in the centre, while the rest of the things were taken upstairs. The operation took little more than an hour. When Mark had tipped the foreman, and shut the front gates, he strolled back to the house.

Janet was upstairs in the room Mark was to use as a study,

already putting his books straight. She wore a smock with huge green and black flowers, had a bandeau about her hair, and was making a businesslike approach to the task.

'Now steady on,' said Mark. 'You mustn't start spoiling me. I'll have to show you I'm still sound in wind and limb, and capable.'

'Capable?' asked Janet reflectively. 'That's a new angle.'

'How Roger stands you I just don't know.' He lit a cigarette and handled a well-thumbed volume of Livy. 'Wasn't he due for a day off?'

'A day!' exclaimed Janet with explosive vehemence. 'He has five weeks and six days' leave owing, half of it from last year. Mark, I'm rather worried.'

'About what?'

'About overwork. Roger hasn't had even a Sunday off for two months, and three times last week he was called out in the middle of the night. I know they're short-handed at the Yard, but there are limits. Haven't you noticed anything odd about him lately?'

Mark considered, not too seriously.

'He's no more moon-eyed than usual. Or should I say moonstruck? You know what young men in love are like.'

'Haven't you noticed his eyes?'

'I know they're beautiful, like the rest of him, but—'

'They're red-rimmed all the time – and he's got more crow's feet in the last few weeks than he ever had before,' declared Janet. 'If he doesn't get a rest, he'll crack. I've threatened twice to go and see Sir Guy, but I don't think Roger would take it too well.'

'You've threatened to see the AC? You're not serious.'

'I'm as serious as you are about your precious pots and pans,' said Janet. 'I tell you that Roger's been working at a silly pace. It wouldn't matter if it were only for a week or two but he's been at the same pressure since Gabby Potter was caught.'

'I can see you're serious,' said Mark, 'but you mustn't beard the lion in his den, even when it's only the Assistant

Commissioner in his study. I've seen that look in your eyes before, but it really wouldn't do. Chatsworth would probably explode so that others heard, and all the Yard would know about it. Roger would never live it down. Can't you imagine it? Handsome's little wifey-pifey protests that Handsome isn't getting a square deal.'

'Roger said the same thing,' complained Janet, 'but something must be done.' She paused, and a knowing look sparked her eyes. 'Mark, you know Sir Guy, and he'll listen to you. Will you have a word with him? You could go to see him about something else.'

Mark eyed her with increasing wariness, said nothing until she had finished, then he waved a hand about the room. 'So now I know what's behind the new lodger. What did I call it – a generous gesture? All you want is to get me completely in your power, and start giving me orders. It would be worth surrendering the whole house to persuade me to interview Sir Guy about Roger's overwork.'

'Don't be ridiculous, Mark.' She picked up a book and banged the pages resonantly, to get the dust off.

'Careful!' exclaimed Mark. He leapt towards her, taking the volume from her hands. 'Jan, my pet, that book has to be treated with reverence. It's a Scott first edition. And don't change the subject. Did you or did you not think of asking me to intercede, before today?'

'Well, yes, but it wouldn't have made any difference. Obviously this was the place for you to come. But I did hope – I mean, *can't* you do anything?'

'Why does it matter?' he asked.

'It's hard to say. Two or three times recently he's had a telephone call and gone out in the middle of the night, but he hasn't been to the Yard. He's told me that's where he's been, but I've learned that he hasn't been to the office, or else arrived a long time after leaving here. It may be something he's been ordered not to tell me, but I can't help feeling that he's trying to save me from being worried.'

'How much do you really know, or think you know?' asked Mark. 'How often have these mysterious telephone messages come in? Where do you think he does go?'

'Answer to the first question, I know nothing. To the second, twice a week for two or three weeks. To the third, I don't know, except that he doesn't go straight to the Yard.'

'Does he know that you know that he doesn't?'

'I don't think so. I usually ask someone at the Yard who won't say anything to him.'

'I'll make three guesses who it is,' said Mark. 'Sergeant Sloan, Sergeant William Sloan, or Old Bill. Doesn't he know the answers?'

'He says he doesn't,' said Janet. 'Don't get Sloan into trouble, Mark.'

'I won't. You know, it's probably some undercover job, and Roger's the most likely man to handle it. In a few weeks it'll all be over, and he'll probably be able to tell you something about it.'

Janet eyed him for a long time, and then said clearly: 'If he doesn't get a few days off this week, I'm going to see Sir Guy. I wish—hush!' She broke off, and Mark listened. A moment later there was a footstep downstairs, and a hearty: 'Anyone at home?' Janet spoke swiftly. 'Not a word. And look at him carefully when you come down.'

She was gone in a flash, and Mark stared at the partly open door as she hurried down the stairs. He did not go to the landing for some minutes, until conversation floated up from downstairs. He gathered that Roger had missed lunch. He had been delayed unexpectedly, but was free until the morning – unless anything unexpected cropped up.

Mark fancied there was a note of weariness in his friend's voice, or, if not weariness, a note foreign to it. Jaded was better, although Roger West was not a man to get easily jaded.

If he were keeping official secrets under his hat, there was no likelihood that he would unburden himself to a friend any more than to his wife. On the other hand, in some cases which had proved difficult and frustrating, he had discussed the issues with Mark, although keeping Janet in the dark, to save her from worrying.

When the voices stopped, Mark stepped to the landing. He heard Roger in the hall, whistling with a gaiety which sounded strained. There was no spring in his step as he mounted the stairs.

Then Roger West, as tall as Mark, fair-haired, good-looking enough to merit the nickname 'Handsome' at the Yard, saw Mark. His face cleared, he stopped whistling, and raised a hand.

'So you've made it. Anything broken?'

'My faith,' said Mark, and did not enlarge.

'In what?' demanded Roger, stopping by the open bathroom door. The light was good, and there was plenty of evidence of lack of sleep in Roger's red-rimmed grey eyes. There were a myriad of tiny lines, too, which he had never noticed before; they gave the impression that Roger was getting old.

'What are you looking like that for?'

'I've seen some odd contrasts in my life, but this afternoon is the first time I've seen a man frowning while he whistles. They never seem to go together.'

'Don't be an ass,' said Roger irritably. 'I'll have a wash, and see you in a few minutes.'

Roger came into Mark's room a little while later, and surveyed the mess, smiling and more himself.

'We'll come up and give you a hand as soon as we've finished lunch,' said Roger.

'You'll do nothing of the kind,' declared Mark. 'I've seen the barbarian hand of Janet amongst the books already. You go out for a nice walk, or lounge in the garden, and have some tea for me in a couple of hours. You don't get much time off. Spend what little you have with Janet.'

'We'll be up,' said Roger.

He was wrong: an hour later Mark, buried in his task but pondering over the peculiar situation between Janet and

Roger, started abruptly at a faint squeaking sound behind him. He swung round, a duster in one hand, a book in the other. Janet, her forefinger at her lips, tiptoed in. *'He's asleep.'*

'Good.'

'He just sat down after lunch, and started to fill his pipe, but he was asleep before it was alight. He is too tired. I'm not going to let it go on any longer. He won't listen to reason, and stay away from the office for a few days. Either you'll see Sir Guy, or I will.'

Mark rubbed his bony chin. 'An ultimatum?'

'Expiring at six o'clock tonight,' Janet said. 'It may be all my eye and Betty Martin, but I'm not going to see Roger crack up in front of my eyes without trying to do something about it. Shall I ring Sir Guy for an appointment, or will you?'

Caller

'I THINK IT'S the craziest notion that even you've had for a long time, but if someone has to see Chatsworth it had better be me. I'll phone Chatsworth right away,' promised Mark. 'You make sure that Roger doesn't wake up and find out what I'm doing. My life won't be worth living if he does.'

Mark went downstairs and into the lounge, where the telephone stood on a small table by a fireplace filled with fir cones. He dialled Chatsworth's private number and was answered by a suave-voiced servant.

'I'm sorry, sir. Sir Guy is out of town.'

Mark felt a spark of hope. 'When will he be back?'

'He has a luncheon appointment here tomorrow, sir.'

'I'll call again tomorrow,' said Mark. 'Tell him I called, please – my name is Mark Lessing. He'll know me.'

As he replaced the receiver, Janet tiptoed into the room. 'So long as you do see him,' she said. 'Mark dear, I'm so grateful.'

Just before five o'clock, when Mark's room was as straight as it could be, the telephone bell rang. Janet went downstairs to answer it.

'Anyone for me?' Roger called, still half-asleep.

'Mrs Elliott, asking us to bridge tonight,' answered Janet. 'I told her we would be too busy settling our lodger in.' She made a moue at Mark, who saw Roger's relaxation and was impressed by yet another demonstration of his friend's tension. Nothing was said; Roger went upstairs to change his shoes, and Janet made tea.

In the kitchen, Mark asked: 'You haven't any plans for tonight, have you?'

'No,' said Janet. 'Why?'

'I thought if Roger and I were here together, I might induce him to take the brakes off. I mean, it's just possible he'll unburden himself.'

'It's not a bad idea,' said Janet thoughtfully. 'I'm going out after tea for an hour. Hush.'

'Now what's the conspiracy about?' demanded Roger from the door.

He looked rested, the redness had gone from his eyes, although the crow's feet still remained. He yawned several times during tea, which they had in a small loggia at the back of the house to the accompaniment of radio music from three different sets, all tuned into different stations, and occasional outburst from the child-cum-mongrel-cum-dustbin lid next door.

'While you two are listening to the news,' Janet said just before six o'clock, 'I'll slip in next door.'

'Arrange for the demise of that ghastly child for me, will you?' asked Mark.

'He's a nice boy.' Janet kissed the top of Roger's head. 'Don't doze off again, darling, or you won't sleep tonight.'

Mark tuned in the radio, which was in the lounge, and music came softly, and soon the *peeps* of the Greenwich time signal sounded clearly.

'I'll turn it up a bit,' said Roger.

The news was of murders and taxes and production needs. As the announcer went on, Roger said abruptly: 'Has Janet told you?'

'Eh? Told me what?'

'I'm not sure that I can trust you,' said Roger. 'I wouldn't put it behind the pair of you to get into a huddle. About my frequent night calls.'

'She *did* mention something about it,' admitted Mark, as if trying to recall what Janet had said. 'She thinks you're overdoing it, and between you and me, you don't look as fresh as a daisy.'

'I'm busier than I want to be,' Roger admitted. 'But it can't be helped, and it's hush-hush. Try to reassure her, will you? I don't like to think that she's worried.'

'For what it's worth, I'll try,' said Mark. 'If she starts taking any serious notice of me, that will be the day. I suppose I can't be your Watson? Humble servant, earnest disciple, and all that kind of thing. I mean, if I can be of any help, just say the word.'

'Not this time, Mark. Sorry.'

'Oh, I don't expect to do more than pick up a few crumbs from the master's table,' said Mark humbly. 'If the situation should alter, though, pass on the word and I'll come frisking up.'

Janet did not come in until after seven o'clock, and then went to make omelettes for supper. Between Mark and Roger there remained a companionable silence, one which had often existed between them.

Mark did some more unpacking before going to bed, and dropped off quickly. He had no idea what time it was when something woke him up.

It was the high-pitched *burr-burr* of a telephone. There was an extension, and a bell, in the Wests' bedroom, adjoining this room. It seemed to ring interminably, and Mark would not have been surprised to learn that Janet was refusing to answer and Roger too sound asleep to be awakened.

Instead, there was a break in the ringing, but it soon started again. Then Roger's voice sounded: 'Hallo, what's that?' He was gruff. 'Oh, damn the thing. All right, sweet.' The bell stopped ringing. After a brief wait, the ting! of the instrument being replaced reached Mark's ears, and was followed by Janet's protesting: 'Roger, not again.'

Roger said something, persuasively. Soon there was a creaking noise. Then something fell with an ominous clatter, enough to have awakened Mark had he been asleep; it sounded like the alarm clock falling. There was a confused murmur of voices, and Roger said something which sounded like: 'You'll wake Mark.' Mark grinned to himself, climbed out of bed, and groped for his clothes.

There was a chill in the night air, but by the time he had on slacks, a pullover, and rubber-soled shoes, he felt much warmer. He had left his cigarettes, matches, and small change in his coat pocket, and slipped the coat on as the other door opened. Roger's footsteps passed his door.

Mark went to the door, and opened it a few inches. There was Janet, in a dressing gown. She whispered: 'Are you awake?'

'I'll follow him.' Then a thought struck him. 'But will he go by car?'

'He doesn't usually,' said Janet.

The front door opened and closed, and all was quiet except for Mark's footsteps down the stairs. He opened the front door and stepped to the porch. It was colder here than in his bedroom, and he shivered as he walked along the drive. He could not hear Roger's footsteps then, and assumed that Roger also had rubber-soled shoes.

To the right, towards King's Road, there was a faint glow of a torch, presumably Roger's. Mark hurried along, but began to wonder whether he was making a fool of himself. A police car might be waiting at the end of the road. Sergeant 'Old Bill' Sloan had deliberately misled Janet.

Roger turned right again, into King's Road.

When Mark reached the corner there was no torch shining, but he was just able to discern Roger's figure, twenty yards or more ahead of him. The light was better; dawn was breaking. That put the time at about four-thirty.

Two lorries rumbled past him, and three others came towards him, but Roger did not stop and was not picked up. He was striding along without glancing behind, apparently oblivious to the fact that he was being followed. When he passed over the railway bridge into Chelsea, he crossed the road and took a side street towards the Thames. Two or three people were about, and some cyclists came along.

Roger reached the Embankment.

By then the light was so good that Mark slackened his pace, for a glance would reveal him, and he did not think that Roger would be appreciative of his presence.

Roger walked along the Embankment, close to the parapet. The Thames was at high tide, and some heavily-laden barges were moving down river. To the left the stark shape of the Albert Bridge, its skeleton-like suspension spans showing clearly against the sky, was approached by occasional vehicles. Mark kept to the other side of the road.

Then at first innocently enough, two men came from a turning farther along, and crossed the road. They walked quickly, with long strides, and they were both tall. Their features were indistinct, but one walked with a limp, going down on his left side with every other step. It did not appreciably slow him down. Both of them reached the Embankment a few yards behind Roger, who did not look round.

Mark quickened his pace.

He did not do so because he thought that there would be need for him; he took advantage of the cover offered by the strangers. In spite of the quickening of his pace, however, Mark was twenty yards behind Roger and on the other side of the road, when the two men broke into a run.

They were going to attack Roger.

'Look out!' Mark bellowed.

Roger swung round into a blow from the man with the limp, who was carrying a weapon; Mark saw his arm rise. Roger seemed to avoid the full force of it, but the second man leapt to the attack.

Mark was rushing along, as a car came along the road.

The driver blew urgently upon his horn. Mark hesitated, glanced about, and saw the oncoming car swerving outwards towards the crown of the road. If he ran on he would run into it. He dodged back. The brakes squealed, and the car driver leaned forward. 'Feel like suicide, mate?'

Mark gasped: 'Sorry!' and darted round the back.

He could hardly believe his eyes.

Roger was being lifted towards the parapet, one man carrying his legs, the other his shoulders. His body was limp. Mark shouted again, and the driver said: *'Strewth.'* Still fifteen yards behind the assailants, Mark saw them swing Roger over the parapet and into the river.

'My God!' muttered Mark. 'He'll drown!' He half-turned and signalled towards the men who were running along the Embankment, hoping that the motorist would give chase. He heard the snarl of the self-starter as he reached the point where Roger had been thrown in. He tore his coat off, and dropped it to the pavement, climbed the parapet, and dived in.

He could see Roger, a few yards away from him, floating on his face, *sinking*. He struck out, desperately, reached Roger, turned him on his back and kept him afloat. He did not like the pallor of Roger's face or his slack lips, with dirty Thames water seeping out at the corners.

Someone shouted from the parapet. A rope fell close to him. Suddenly help appeared to come from three or four places at once. Men moved in all directions, and a small police launch chugged-chugged towards the spot. Two men leaned over, caught hold of Roger, and hauled him aboard.

An elderly river policeman said: 'Blimey, that's Handsome West.'

Other willing hands were clutching at Mark, and helping him over the parapet and back to the Embankment. He would have preferred to go with Roger, but there was nothing he could do about it. The chill of the soaking started his teeth chattering, and some well-intentioned idiot thought that he needed artificial respiration, when all he needed was to get warm.

He was taken across the road to a ground floor flat, a hot bath, and a change of clothes. Within the hour he was almost himself.

He left the flat at a little after six o'clock. A telephone inquiry to Scotland Yard got him nowhere, and he went along to the nearest jetty. There an old man dressed in bulky rags, and with a week-old stubble on a nutcracker jaw, told him that the river 'narks' had brought someone out of the river. And: 'Whyn't they let 'im drahn, that's wot I want t'know,' he droned. 'Whyn't they let 'im drahn? Poor swab, wanted t'do 'isself in, didn't 'e? Whyn't they let 'im drahn?'

The motorist who had nearly run Mark down appeared, a portly man who was still excited. He had seen them take 'him' – meaning Mark – to the flat, and hurried along to see how the 'victim' was. He had not seen any more than the old man, who stood mumbling to himself. What an amazing business it was, declared the garrulous one. And how he wished he had thought to follow the two men who had thrown the 'victim' into the river.

'I certainly wish you had,' Mark said.

'Thrown 'im?' gasped the derelict. He stared from one to the other, then hunched his shoulders and assumed an expression of woebegone despair. 'Yer couldn't spare a bob, mister, could yer? Give me a n'appetite, that 'as.'

Mark looked at him thoughtfully, and jingled coins in his pocket. Before he took any out, he asked pertinent questions. Apparently the old man had slept on a seat on the Embankment. He had been awakened by shouting, and by men rushing past him.

Mark said sharply: 'Did you see them clearly?'

'Nark it, Guv'ner. Me eyes weren't 'ardly open. No one brings *me* a cuppa tea ter see I'm awake on the dot, see.'

'Would you recognise either of them again?' insisted Mark.

The motorist was eager, now. The old man's rheumy, cunning eyes, small and very blue, were close to Mark's face.

'I couldn't swear I would, Guv'ner, but I *might*. They 'adn't got none of wot the cops call distingershing marks, but one o' them had a bad leg, I know that, 'e limped.'

'At least he's telling the truth about that,' Mark thought.

Aloud, he said: 'If you saw that much, you must have seen their faces.'

'Just faces, thassall,' said the derelict. 'I might recognise them again, but I couldn't be sure. I don't 'old wiv false pertences, Guv'ner. Besides, the dicks is planning an identerfication parade, ain't they? That on yer mind?'

'It could be,' agreed Mark. 'Where can I find you again?'

'I dunno that you can,' the derelict said. ''Ere today, gone tomorrow, that's me. It ain't *my* fault. This ain't a bad pitch and I'd stay as long as the perishin' narks would let me. Two nights, *if* I'm lucky, an' tonight's the second.'

Mark took out a handful of silver coins.

'Be here at twelve o'clock tomorrow morning, and I'll double this.' He dropped three half-crowns, a two-shilling piece, and a sixpence into a grimy palm, heard a gratified thanks, and turned on his heel. The man might keep the appointment out of avarice, but fear of the police would probably persuade him to be satisfied with what he had made.

The motorist hurried in Mark's wake, protesting peevishly that he had decided to try to help him get the other man out of the river; he hadn't known that so many people would be at hand. He was sorry that he had not followed the assailants. Was there anything he could do to make amends?

'You can run me home,' he said pleasantly.

'That'll be a pleasure, that's quite all right,' the fat one assured him. He had a reddish face and needed a shave, but his blue eyes were wide open and earnest. 'Is it far?'

'About a mile and a half.'

'Oh, that's *no* trouble.'

Mark sat with him, and listened to his apologies. He could kick himself for letting the men get away, he had not even noticed which turning they had taken, and the worst of it was that he could have caught up with them easily.

Mark was more concerned for Roger than with the escape of his assailants, and at the back of his mind there was reluctance to tell Janet what had happened; at least he could assure her that Roger had not been badly hurt. But she would realise the assailants had knocked Roger out and tossed him into the river to drown.

'It's the next turning, thanks,' he said to the driver. 'Drop me here, and I'll walk the rest.'

Now the moment for seeing Janet was on him. He turned the corner, and saw an ambulance outside Roger's house.

Interview

THE ENGINE OF the ambulance started as Mark walked towards it. It moved off. Outside the gate stood a policeman, stolid and stalwart. His white summer-issue gloves made him a clear outline against his tunic. Most of the men in this Division, as well as the Yard, knew 'Handsome's' friend, Mr Lessing. Many made cracks about the amateur, but most held him in some respect.

'Good morning, sir.'

'Morning,' said Mark. 'Nice to know you're here.' He went up to the front door, hand outstretched for the bell before he remembered that he had a key. He pushed the Yale into the lock, turned it, and went inside.

Women's voices sounded from the kitchen. Mark went towards it as the door opened and a middle-aged nurse appeared. She stopped short, and gasped. Janet appeared by her side.

'Thank heavens *you're* all right!' She sounded genuinely relieved. 'This is Mr Lessing, nurse,' she went on briskly. 'He is staying with us.'

The nurse turned big, bright grey eyes towards Mark. Her face was gaunt and lined, her lips compressed. She nodded curtly, and passed on. Mark took Janet's arm. 'How is he?'

'If he'd gone out on his own, I wouldn't have been surprised at this,' said Janet, 'but I thought you were going to look after him. How on earth did you let it happen?'

Mark squeezed her arm. 'I'm not so quick as I thought I was.

Things moved too fast. How is he?'

'Not *too* bad, I suppose. He's still unconscious, and the doctor says it's concussion. He has some nasty bruises on the side of his head, and – oh, he'll be all right. But this proves I was right. He wouldn't have let it happen if he hadn't been so tired.'

'If we look on the bright side—'

'Have you been hit over the head too?' asked Janet tartly.

'There is a bright side,' insisted Mark. 'You've got him away from the office, and ought to be able to work your will on the doctor to get him declared unfit. There isn't the slightest reason why you shouldn't go off with him to somewhere in the country. He won't be fit enough to argue for a few days, and when he's away he'll be less inclined to want to come back.'

He saw the dawning of understanding in Janet's eyes.

'While he's away the Yard will have to look after things, and by the time Roger's back on duty it may all be over.'

Janet backed into the bright kitchen, and leaned against the edge of the table, eyeing him speculatively. 'I know just the place. I'll telephone Paula now.'

'Does Paula get up in time to hear the seven o'clock news, too?' asked Mark mildly.

'Seven? Great Scott, I didn't realise it was so early,' said Janet, and she eyed him with a new interest. 'What have you been up to?' she demanded suspiciously. 'Where did you get that suit? It doesn't even fit you, and that's a patch on the knee, isn't it?'

'Wait until you see the seat,' said Mark. He told her what had happened. 'If there could be a cup of tea—'

'Of course. I'll put the kettle on.'

At breakfast Janet was full of her friend Paula and a country cottage. He left her to work in his room, unpacking the case of china and putting the precious pieces in the cabinets which had been brought from his flat. The task unfinished, near lunchtime, he heard the front door bell ring. A glance out of his window told him that it was the doctor.

Earlier in the morning Roger had recovered consciousness, but did not remember what had happened, and nurse had refused more than a brief visit by Janet. The doctor's voice now rumbled loudly in the next room, suggesting that he was not set against conversation. After a while he went downstairs. Mark followed, standing behind him while he told Janet that Roger needed complete rest for at least several days.

Janet said, meekly, that the rest was so difficult in Bell Street. There were noises from the neighbours, wireless sets were always blaring, the Yard wouldn't leave him alone.

The doctor, a chunky-faced man whom Mark did not know, prescribed a change of air as soon as practicable; provided care was exercised, he said, there was no reason why Roger should not be moved the following day.

When the doctor had gone, Janet said joyfully: *'That's settled, and Paula would love to have us. Chatsworth can't argue, can he?'*

Mark went by bus to Victoria, where Chatsworth had his flat. On the way, he glanced behind him several times, half-afraid of being followed. He saw nothing to make him suspicious, yet the idea persisted. When he reached the block of flats in St James' Square he sauntered along for some minutes. Then he went into the main entrance, but did not go farther at once.

Two men passed the entrance, going towards the park.

He recognised neither, but noticed them with particular care before going by the empty porter's cubicle to the second floor. He had visited the AC before, and knew the flats well.

The servant who had answered him on the previous evening was a black-dressed robot, an ex-policeman with one hand. Obviously Mark was expected; he was asked to wait in a small and charming lounge. Chatsworth was a bachelor, but there was nothing in the flat to suggest the absence of a woman's touch.

'If you will please come with me, sir,' said the servant a few minutes later. 'Sir Guy is free now.'

Chatsworth was a big man. There were many who said that he looked more like a prosperous country doctor than a policeman who had gone to the Yard fresh from the War Office. To his staff he was something of an enigma, and he often stirred uneasiness in Roger West's mind, although in Mark's opinion Roger was overawed by his chief less than many at the Yard. It was Chatsworth's fancy to have his study at the flat an exact replica of that at Scotland Yard; the room seemed to be nothing but chromium and ebony, or a shiny imitation.

Sitting behind his desk, as if receiving a subordinate at the Yard, Chatsworth overflowed a swivel armchair. A fringe of grizzled hair like a halo round his head emphasised the baldness of the centre. His wide smile had a 'come-into-my-parlour' benevolence which had been the downfall of many who had attempted to deceive. It was said at Scotland Yard that if Chatsworth was amiable he was at his most dangerous; he very nearly purred.

He half-rose from his chair, and extended a big hand. 'Come in, Lessing, come in. It's nice to see you again, very nice.' His grip was powerful. 'Sit down.' He pushed cigarettes and a lighter across his flat-topped and shiny desk, and then relaxed, clasping his hands together like a priest about to pronounce a benign blessing on a bridegroom who had come to arrange for the banns. 'Now, what's worrying you?'

Mark raised his eyebrows.

'Worrying *me?* Does anything, ever?'

'All right, have it your own way. What makes you want to come worrying me?'

'Oh, a general desire to see how you were getting on,' said Mark airily. 'I didn't expect to be received in the *sanctum sanctorum.* I feel almost like a suspect.' He smiled widely. 'How are you, sir? Sleeping well? Pulse quite steady? Not working yourself to a standstill, like some people I know.' His manner robbed the words of offensiveness. He saw Chatsworth's blue eyes narrow, in puzzlement.

'You know, Lessing, I do believe that you're more eccentric

than ever.' Chatsworth's smile was a shade more taut, something of his geniality ebbed.

'Oh, no,' said Mark emphatically. 'I'm always myself. Roger West *is* overdoing it, you know. Or he was. And it isn't like you to overwork anyone deliberately and with malice.'

'I see,' said Chatsworth. 'And what prompted you to come and see me about Roger West? Do you imagine that he would approve of the visit?'

'He'd jump out of his grave if he were as dead as he might be. Seriously, Sir Guy, is it necessary? I know that he's out of action for a little while, but he isn't likely to stay in his room a minute longer than he has to. We've been friends for quite a time. I don't like seeing him cracking up, and that's what's happening. There's even worse.' He paused for effect. 'There's a strained atmosphere at his home, and that's not nice to live with. You know Mrs West, don't you?'

'Does Mrs West know you're here?'

'It isn't a subject for family discussion – the strain, I mean – but it's there, and I don't like it. The thing is, you wouldn't need to overwork Roger if there wasn't something pressing.' He paused. 'I don't like to think of your men being out at all hours, or laid up with concussion, because you're short of personnel.'

There was a change in Chatsworth's expression. He smiled blandly as he leaned back in his chair, nodding so that his one heavy chin became three smaller ones. 'If you want to become a policeman,' said Chatsworth, 'why don't you make the usual application?'

'Oh,' said Mark, shaken. 'You mean fill in forms, and that sort of thing? I suppose I could, but isn't there an age limit? Or are you so short-staffed that you've had to dispense with it?'

Chatsworth widened his eyes, stared for a moment, and then chuckled. Mark had feared for a moment that he had gone further than he should; to have Chatsworth hostile would do no good.

'Lessing,' said Chatsworth, 'you are no fool. But, you know, there are things I can't do. Sometimes West has talked to you about his cases, and in his reports has even said that you have been of some help. Although I can turn a blind eye to some irregularities, there are limits, and clearly defined ones. You haven't discussed this with West, have you?'

'Haven't I, though? I spent thirty seconds yesterday afternoon offering to be his Watson, but was turned down flat. Hush-hush, and all that kind of thing, he said. When I was about to press for more, he—' Mark paused.

'Well?'

'He fell asleep,' said Mark. 'That's what really made me decide to come here. If Roger can fall asleep in the middle of telling me that he can't tell me anything, he's at the end of his tether. As I was staying at the house last night, I heard the phone go, and I followed him. And I—'

'I've heard all about that,' said Chatsworth.

'You hear about everything, don't you?'

'Very nearly,' said Chatsworth. 'And I think you probably saved his life. You were very prompt.'

'Prompt?' Mark grinned. 'I went at a snail's pace, or he wouldn't have been tossed over the parapet. Incidentally, one of the men who attacked him had a limp, and both were tall. There was also a tramp nearby, who saw them running. I have an appointment with him for noon tomorrow, and I hope he'll be on hand when you stage the identification parade.'

'You seem sure we'll get the men,' said Chatsworth.

'Well, won't you?'

'Oh, eventually, of course, eventually. Now, Lessing, it's time we stopped beating about the bush. I understand your concern and I don't underrate you, but I can imagine no way in which you can assist us in this case. West was quite right to say nothing to you. He was simply carrying out instructions. I'm sorry, but there is no way in which I can use your services. If there were, I would.' He paused to allow that to sink in. 'Having so decided, I must impress upon you the need for discretion. In fact—' he leaned forward again, looking very earnest, and repeated: 'In fact, I hope you will give me your assurance that you will not endeavour to take a personal interest in the affair. Will you do that, Mr Lessing?'

Mr Lessing is Insistent

SOME SECONDS passed before Mark actually uttered 'no'.

Then it came with conviction, bald and clear. Chatsworth sat back, and after a silence which seemed longer than it was, he said: 'You are extremely foolish. I am reluctant to do more than tell you that you are to take no further part in this matter without the express approval of a responsible officer under my control. Is that clearly understood?'

'I think so.'

'I trust it is. And I trust that you will take my advice,' said Chatsworth. 'If you don't, I will not be responsible for the consequences, and I will certainly not guarantee your continued freedom of movement.'

Mark stared. 'I didn't quite get that last one.'

'You will, if you think about it,' said Chatsworth. 'Good evening, Mr Lessing.'

Somewhat surprisingly, he shook hands. A few moments afterwards Mark found himself standing outside the door of the flat, which the one-armed servant closed.

Mark brushed a hand over his forehead and walked to the stairs, and down into the street. He was so preoccupied with thought of Chatsworth's manner, and his abrupt dismissal, that he quite forgot to keep his eyes open for the two men whom he had noticed earlier. He decided to take a turn round the park, in the hope of collecting himself and really facing the seriousness of Chatsworth's purpose. Actually the last thrust had been obvious enough, and there was hardly any need to think about it. Chatsworth had told him that if he interfered he might be detained.

'He did give me a loophole,' Mark mused. 'I can act with the approval of a responsible Yard man. But of course all of them will be told not to play. Now I wonder what it's all about.'

He had a snack supper at a little French restaurant, before walking back to Fulham. Dusk was gathering, and the plain-clothes men outside the Wests' house loomed massive and forbidding, despite the fact that they acknowledged him with outward respect.

Indoors, Janet was reading. She put her book down when he entered. Roger was asleep; he had been awake, however, and rational, and there was every prospect of him being moved tomorrow. Chatsworth had telephoned just after Mark had left, to say that he was providing an ambulance and that Roger was not to be in a hurry to get back to work.

'And of course, you agreed,' said Mark gloomily.

'I told him I wouldn't keep him a minute longer than was necessary,' said Janet, with an innocent smile. 'He's rather a dear I suppose. Oh, and Paula wanted to know whether you were free to come, too.'

'Have you been hatching dark deeds on the telephone with your cousin?'

'Nothing of the sort,' said Janet. 'But I *did* tell her you were looking a little run down, and might try to come for the weekend. Please yourself. But why you think Paula is an ogre I can't understand.'

'She's far too possessive for my liking. If she were single I wouldn't go within a hundred miles of her.'

Janet put her head on one side and regarded him with some concern. He stood with an elbow resting against the mantelpiece of the lounge, and scowled down upon her.

'You *are* in a sweet temper,' she remarked. 'Wasn't Chatsworth very friendly?'

'No.'

'What did he say?'

'He warned me off. This business is considered so dangerous that I am not even allowed to hover about the outer fringes. Don't *you* know anything about it?' he demanded with sudden eagerness. 'Hasn't Roger said anything in his sleep, or let out a hint? Damn it, he must have done!'

'He certainly hasn't,' Janet assured him emphatically, 'and it doesn't worry me now. When we're at Paula's, Roger will stay put until it's all over, and if there is more trouble coming to anybody, it won't be to him.' She paused. 'Mark, don't look so sick about it. Why don't you come down to Paula's for the weekend? You'll enjoy it once you're there.'

'I am in no mood to enjoy anything,' Mark said, 'but I probably will. You're a dangerous woman, you know. When you look like that you could melt ice. Perhaps Roger isn't such a fool after all. What time are you leaving?'

'At twelve o'clock, if the doctor says it's all right when he comes again.'

'Good,' said Mark. 'That's one thing off our minds. And now, unless there's anything you want me to do, I'll toddle off to bed.'

'You might bolt the front door as you go up,' said Janet. 'Good night.'

Mark smiled crookedly at her, and then went upstairs. He looked out of his bedroom window, and did not need to concentrate to see the burly figures of two other plain-clothes men in the alley at the end of the garden. Chatsworth was making quite sure that no one attacked Roger, or otherwise made contact with him.

'Chatsworth makes it worse by admitting the possibility,' Mark thought. 'What the blazes is happening?'

As there was no immediate solution he went to bed expecting an uneasy night. Instead, he went to sleep quickly, and was not awakened until Janet entered the room, carrying a tray of tea. He struggled up in bed, inquired after the patient, and was assured that Roger had slept well.

'I haven't slept so soundly for weeks,' said Janet. 'What kind of a night did you have?'

'Terrible.'

'Certainly you don't look too good.' Janet was out of the room before Mark could think of a suitable reply.

He waited until the doctor made his visit, gave a good report, and said that Roger could be moved. Janet was travelling to Dorset with the ambulance, and she repeated the invitation for Mark to follow for the weekend. Mark said that he would telephone one way or the other, and then went to the office. He could not get in to see Roger because of the battleaxe of a nurse. He saw his Chief, who, a few days before, had told him that if he wanted a week's leave this was as good a time as any to take it. Mark disparaged his own position at the Home Office, but had not given up all hope of getting promotion. His knowledge of languages made him invaluable. His Chief said promptly that he could take a week off, and asked what he thought of doing.

'Burying myself in the country for a real rest,' declared Mark.

He would not admit even to himself that he proposed to follow Janet and Roger because he thought that trouble might catch up with them. He did not think for a moment that Paula Dean's home would be free from the attentions of the police; Roger would be guarded as carefully in the Dorset village of Hinton Magna as in Fulham.

He had two suitcases already packed, unopened since he had come to Bell Street, and he telephoned Waterloo to learn that there was a train to Dorchester, via Bournemouth, at 3.25. He was assured that it was a good train; it was due in Dorchester about eight o'clock.

At two-thirty he reached the Bell Street house, collected his cases, and, because taxis were scarce, carried them to King's Road and boarded a bus. As he was standing on the platform, with the conductress impatient about his baggage, a wheezy voice sounded. "Ere, mister. *Mister!*'

There was an urgent, pleading note in the familiar voice. Mark looked over his shoulder, and the conductress pressed the bell.

'Mister!' called the man with the wheezy voice desperately.

It was the tramp whom he had seen on the Embankment.

His clothes were not only ragged but odorous. His week-old stubble was a dirty grey, and his hands were scored and ingrained with dirt. From the depths of his clothes he drew an old, cracked pipe, which was empty. He stared at it gloomily, without saying a word.

Equally silent, Mark offered him a cigarette.

'Ta,' said the old one, as if surprised. And then: 'You're a fine one, aincha. I thought we 'ad an'appointment.'

'We did,' said Mark humbly. 'I'm sorry.'

'Thassal very well, but I was 'angin' around the Embankment for a coupla hours. Supposin' it'd been a cold day, mister? Or a wet one? Where would I 'ave bin then?'

'On the Embankment,' said Mark. 'You're a man of your word, Mr—'

'Eh?'

'I said I didn't quite catch your name.'

'Oh, everyone knows me,' boasted the tramp with great aplomb. 'They calls me Crummy, even the narks. Crummy Parker, that's me.' He looked up with an indescribably cunning gleam in his eyes, albeit with a deliberate, unmistakable humour. 'Thought I was goin' to lose that ten bob, mister, didn't yer?'

'I hadn't given much thought to it,' admitted Mark.

'Well, I ain't see. I was waiting for you at midday, and you know what you promised me.' He was mildly truculent. 'The thing I want to arst you, mister, is how much is it worth to know where the lame cove lives?'

'Parker, I was born long enough ago to know what you're after. I'm not easy money. If I pay anything for the man's address I've got to have proof that he lives there.'

'Wotjer think *I* am?' demanded Parker. 'Old enough to be yer farver, cully, and I'm tellin' you I know when I'm on an easy pickin'. A friend of Inspector West ain't no fool, believe me.'

The admission that he knew that Mark was acquainted with Roger was another in a chain of surprises. He was still trying to absorb it when the conductress shouted that the next stop was Victoria. Mark got up, making a decision quickly. There must be a later train to Dorchester, and if it came to the point he could travel down the next morning.

'We'll talk in the street,' he said.

Parker followed him down the stairs, but did not offer to assist him to lift the two cases off the platform.

Mark felt conspicuous on the pavement opposite the Grosvenor Hotel, although he was not normally self-conscious. The feeling wasn't wholly due to his company; he felt that he was being watched, and had an uneasy suspicion that a man who had jumped from a bus immediately behind his was now walking slowly by, and watching him from the other side of the road.

He stepped against the wall, leaving the bags by the kerb.

'I've just twenty minutes to spare,' he said. 'My train goes at twenty-past three. Now, what's it all about?'

'I've told you,' declared Parker. 'I know where the cove wiv a limp lives, mister. Do you want to know or doncher? I don't care whether you buy or you don't buy.'

'How far does he live from here?'

'Matter've 'arf an hour.'

'How did you find out?'

Parker winked, keeping the lid down for an appreciable time. 'I got me methods.'

'How much do you want for the information?' Mark demanded.

'Twenty quid!'

'Ten,' said Mark.

'Twenty.'

'Ten.'

'Seventeen,' said Parker, now wide-eyed.

'Ten,' insisted Mark firmly.

'Strewth, you're a hard case,' complained Parker aggrievedly.

'Ten quid, for a bit've info' like that. Fifteen, mister. If yer don't want it, I know where I can sell fer that, an' that's a fact.'

'If you thought anyone would pay more than I will, you'd have gone to him first,' said Mark. 'Twelve pounds, and that's my limit.'

'Rob an unborn child, you would,' declared Parker. 'I never met an'arder case, that's a fact. Twelve bloomin' quid, an' – blimey, wot's yer middle name? Flint? Orl right, orl right, twelve quid. Arf dahn, arf later,' he added cunningly. 'That's fair.'

'One pound down, the rest when I know you're not lying.'

'*One* dahn? Now look 'ere, mister, don't come it.'

Parker's expression and tone suggested a deadlock, and Mark shrugged his shoulders and turned to the kerb, looking in either direction as if for a taxi. The tramp stayed by the wall, glaring at his back, until a taxi hove in sight. Before its driver could see Mark's half-raised arm, Parker shuffled forward. 'Orl right, where's the quid?' He waited with outstretched hand for a pound note. 'I can't wait all day, mister. Yer've gotta come wiv me, no catchin' no trains.'

'I'll take my bag to the cloakroom first,' Mark said. 'Lend me a hand, will you?'

He did not take the cases across to Victoria Station wholly because it was most convenient; he was dubious about his companion's honesty of purpose and considered it wise not to make it obvious that he was travelling from Waterloo. If Parker were working for the other side, and this was a put-up job to disarm him, it was best to make the tramp believe that his destination was reached on one of the lines running from Victoria.

Ten minutes passed before the suitcases were in a cloakroom, and the two men stood together outside it. Parker looked up with a slow grin. 'Yer ain't gettin' the wind-up, mister, are yer?'

'Why should I be?' demanded Mark.

'Oh, I dunno, I dunno,' said Parker. 'I was kind've wonderin' if you was thinkin've the way them two coves took hold of the

Inspector. They wasn't very tender wiv 'im, was they?'

'Crummy,' confided Mark slowly, 'I wasn't thinking of Inspector West, or the man with the limp. I was wondering how far you can be trusted.'

'What, *me?*' Parker was affronted. 'You ain't ever 'eard a word against Crummy Parker, I'll betcher.'

For all the man's dirt and obvious avarice there was something likeable about him. At a smile in Mark's eyes, Parker's expression relaxed, and he said: 'Let's get goin', or the bird will 'ave flown. I couldn't sleep a wink tonight if I lorst me extra eleven quid. Battersea, that's where we're goin'. Can yer sport a cab?'

Mark held his hand up towards a taxi.

The taxi driver made no comment, audible or by expression, but leaned out and opened the door. Mark stood aside, and Crummy Parker climbed unsteadily into the cab and sank back in a corner with an expression of serene satisfaction. Through the open glass partition he ordered with lordly air: 'Queen's Street, Battersea. And 'urry, please.'

'Very good, sir,' said the cabby.

'Respect, that's wot I like from a driver,' declared Parker with satisfaction. 'They knows a gentleman when they sees one, which is more'n yer could say for the narks, *an'* some uvver people.' He was silent for a moment, and then added, 'I'll tell yer something. I'm beginning to *like* you. I'll tell yer something else, too, case I get a n'eart attack before we get to Limpy's 'ouse. Thirty-one Queen's Street, Battersea, that's where he lives.'

'I see,' said Mark slowly, and did not show his satisfaction. 'How did you find him?'

Parker stared at him, then leaned forward and spoke swiftly and earnestly.

'Listen, Guv'ner, you're a sport, I can see it. I'll tell yer all of it, every perishing word of it, for another three quid. No secrets, see. That's an offer – what about it?'

'All right, Crummy,' Mark said. 'What's the story?'

His story was certainly plausible, and Mark found it convincing with slight mental reservations.

Parker knew Handsome West by sight; so did most people on London's seamy side, and there was nothing surprising in that. Something had woken him up, and he had been awake when Roger had walked along the Embankment. He had even been considering touching Roger for a cup of tea, but suddenly the attack had developed. Naturally, Parker had done nothing, but he had seen Mark's rescue attempt and much which had followed. After the brief interview, he had 'made inquiries' amongst friends, and learned where Mark had lived. That, he said, was easy: a lot of people knew that 'Handsome' had a friend, and Mr Lessing, begging his pardon, wasn't a man hard to describe.

That was one side of the story, explaining how Parker had come to be near Bell Street. The other was even simpler. Parker had been about amongst his 'friends', mostly unpopular with the police, and described the man with the limp. Identification had been comparatively easy. He had been told of Queen's Street, visited the place that morning, and seen the man enter the house. He was quite sure it was one of Roger's two attackers.

When he finished, Parker leaned back in his corner and demanded: 'How'd yer like the sound of it, mister?'

'It'll do,' said Mark.

As he spoke the cab turned a corner, and slowed down. A quick glance at a street nameplate told Mark they were in Queen's Street, and then the taxi slowed down outside number 35. Mark climbed out, Parker followed him, and Mark was taking some change from his pocket to pay the driver when a dark shadow loomed over him. He looked up, to see a man with a familiar face near him, and another man approaching Parker. The second man he recognised as from Scotland Yard, a sober, red-faced officer who put his hand on Parker's shoulder and said: 'I want you, Parker.'

Mark waited, expecting a hand to descend upon his shoulder.

Sir Guy is Fatherly

HAD MARK been less obsessed with the likelihood of his own arrest, he would have paid more attention to Crummy Parker, who stared into the face of the man who held him, his lips twisted and his eyes buried so that they looked like little slits. Parker gave the impression that he was trying to find words, but the physical and mental effort was too much for him. His breathing grew laboured, and he began to shiver.

'Wotjer mean?' he demanded. 'Wotjer mean? I ain't done nuffink, mister, nuffink at all.'

'Haven't you?' said the police officer.

'I was just 'aving a ride wiv my friend Mr Lessing, that's all.' He drew a deep breath and then appealed to Mark. ''Ave I done anyfink that the bees can take me for?'

'Not—not to my knowledge,' said Mark.

'There you are,' declared Parker, in high-pitched triumph. 'Wotjer want me for, that's wot I wanter know?'

'You've been warned a dozen times,' the CID man said. 'You'll be charged with begging, *and* I wouldn't be surprised if there aren't other charges.'

'Beggin'!' exclaimed Parker. 'Beggin'! Strewth, if that ain't the bloomin' limit. Beggin'! *Me!*'

'Yes, you,' said the officer. 'There are limits to what we'll take from you, Parker. Come on.'

He turned, and with a hand about the tramp's wrist, led him towards the end of the street.

Mark's heart had steadied in the past few minutes, although

he remained uneasy. The fact that nothing had been said to him meant little; if he moved away, he might be detained. To fill an awkward gap he took out his cigarette case and proffered it. Although he recognised the man as a Yard officer, he did not know his name.

'No thanks,' said the man stiffly. 'I'd like—'

He did not finish what he was going to say, for Mark, who was glancing over his shoulder towards the end of the street, saw a tall, well-built man crossing the road. There was something familiar about the fellow, who went down heavily on his left foot. For a split second Mark stared, his expression strained enough to make the Yard man stop speaking. Then he said sharply: 'There's your man! Get him!'

He made a dive past the policeman, going towards the man with the limp who had come from one of the houses at the end of the street, and was moving towards the corner. He did not look round, but moved swiftly, half-running, half-walking, and making his limp more pronounced. There was scant hope of catching him up unless he ran at full speed, and he was about to lengthen his stride when a hand descended upon his shoulder, and he lost his balance. He staggered, tried to shake the hand off, but failed. It was the Yard man, who said sharply: 'That's enough, sir!'

'Don't be an ass!' exclaimed Mark urgently. 'That's the fellow who put West into the river this morning. You must get him. It's vital!'

'*Who* do you say it is?' The fresh-faced officer looked startled, but did not move.

'West's assailant,' cried Mark. 'Are you going to let him go? He's round the corner already.'

The Yard man released him then, as if convinced of the seriousness of the need for giving chase, and outpaced him towards the end of the street, disappearing in the same direction as the man with the limp. When Mark reached the corner, however, he saw the officer standing at a junction of four roads, obviously unable to decide which one his quarry had taken. Mark drew up with him, and said with withering sarcasm: 'That's one step up the ladder you don't get.'

'We've lost him,' the other said, impervious to sarcasm. 'I didn't realise what you meant at first, sir. Had you said "Inspector" West I would have understood you. Still, it can't be helped.'

'What remarkable brilliance there is in the police force,' growled Mark. 'Why, you—'

'I don't think it's necessary to talk about it,' said the officer crisply. 'I was going to tell you—'

'Just what's in your mind, officer?'

'I have instructions to take you to Cannon Row, sir,' said the detective blandly.

Cannon Row was the police station where suspects and others detained for interrogation at the Yard were held. They stepped together into the darkened hall of the police station, went through three doors, and then along a narrow passage: there were other doors leading from the passage, but all of them were barred. They were the cells.

'What is this nonsense?' snapped Lessing.

'I'm only carrying out instructions,' said the officer amiably. 'This way, please.'

Further protest then was useless, Mark knew, and he stepped into a cell some eight feet square. It was not pleasant, and the bleakness of the three walls and the bars which separated it from the passage did nothing to help.

The door closed on him, and the constable turned a key in the lock.

'Well—I'm—damned!' he exploded.

It was only in the next half-hour that he fully realised what had happened, and where this might lead. He thought of his cases at Victoria Station, and the 3.35 from Waterloo. What a damned fool he had been! If he had not seen Crummy Parker he would have been well on the way to Bournemouth, and with the prospect of a week-end at picturesque Hinton Magna ahead of him.

He judged that it was seven o'clock when a man appeared in the cell corridor and walked along it sharply. A plain-clothes man passed his cell and spoke in undertones to the policeman, who entered after a few moments, unlocking the door.

Mark said nothing.

'Will you come this way, please?' asked the plain-clothes man, shorter and more thickset than Mark's first acquaintance.

'I certainly will,' said Mark heavily.

He was led out of Cannon Row into the precincts of Scotland Yard, and along the stone passages and up the lift to the third floor, where Chatsworth had his office. He began to wonder whether Chatsworth had deliberately allowed him to cool his heels, in the belief that he would not take the risk of further detention. It would be like the AC, who might even pretend that his words had been taken too literally by his men. Withholding judgement, but in no amiable frame of mind, Mark waited while his guard tapped on Chatsworth's door and opened it on a mellow 'come in'.

The man stood aside for Mark to enter, and said: 'Mr Lessing, sir. Is there anything else?'

'Not now,' said Chatsworth shortly.

Mark wondered what the opening gambit would be, and was taken by surprise when Chatsworth looked up abruptly. 'Well, Lessing. Have you had enough?'

'More than enough of some things,' he said. 'Police incompetence amongst them. One of your officers stood within twenty yards of a man who helped to throw West into the river. The best he could do was to give the fellow plenty of time for getting away. If he had not been instructed to keep so careful an eye on me, you would have had that man under lock and key by now.'

Chatsworth said: 'Competence or incompetence by my men will be judged by me.'

'Don't forget the Home Secretary,' said Mark sharply. 'Or the Press, or the general public.'

Very slowly Chatsworth leaned back in his chair, took off his glasses, put them on the desk in front of him, and said softly: 'That's to be your attitude, is it?'

Then, without warning, Chatsworth smiled. It was a benign smile, warming, friendly, conciliatory. 'I wish you were in a more amenable frame of mind,' said Chatsworth, 'but I can't hope to alter you.' He chuckled again, but then without warning his expression changed, and he leaned forward over his desk, looking very earnest. 'Lessing, I *will* tell you this. You will be in considerable danger if you ignore my advice, danger from other sources than the police. In fact I can envisage circumstances in which you would be happy to think that you were in the comparative comfort of a cell at Cannon Row. Be warned by me. Don't try to pursue your inquiries.'

'That's easy to say,' said Mark shortly.

Chatsworth shrugged. 'Of course, I can't *make* you take the sensible course, but I strongly advise it. I must leave it to you.'

'That's a concession, anyhow,' Mark said.

He did not think that Chatsworth looked particularly pleased when he reached the door. Whatever lay behind this, he was worried. Probably, too, in order to try to impress him, he had gone too far with Mark. Instead of being chastened, Mark felt much more cheerful. His freedom was a thing of great importance: it was as well not to tell Chatsworth that he would be more careful in the future.

'As far as I can be,' he mused as he entered Parliament Square after receiving respectful salutes from policemen in the hall and at the gates, 'I owe a lot to Crummy Parker. I wonder why they did collar him. And why he talked after all?'

He dismissed thought of Crummy with a half-hearted decision to do what he could to help the tramp later, and then deliberated on the wisdom of returning to Bell Street, or putting up at a hotel for the night. He decided to go to Bell Street.

It was nearly ten o'clock, and dusk was falling, when he reached Bell Street.

He inserted his key in the lock of the front door, pushed the door open, and stepped inside. As he did so Janet's cat came bounding from the next-door garden, and rubbed himself on Mark's legs. Mark leaned down and ruffled the cat's fur, and the cat purred contentedly.

It was when Mark was straightening up that he saw the man on the stairs; a tall, heavily-built man – the man with the limp.

The Vanity of Count Riordon

MARK STOOD on the threshold for what seemed a long time. The other, taken completely by surprise, stood quite still and stared at him. There was no light on in the hall, but the daylight was good enough for Mark to see every feature of the other man clearly.

The man with the limp had broad, rugged features, and a peculiar, square-shaped mouth. His eyes were large, and very cold: even in the half-light, they appeared to glitter. Sinister was the word. And the cat presumably agreed, for it turned and bounded off.

The moment of appraisal passed swiftly. Then he and the man on the stairs moved at the same time. Mark leapt forward to tackle, the other put his right hand to his pocket. Mark saw fleetingly that he would have no chance at all if the other had a gun and fired from his pocket. Then he saw the man draw out a weapon, and raise it: a truncheon of sorts, thought Mark, and moved his head to one side as he quickened his rush.

The other guessed what he would do, and judged his blow accordingly. The weapon caught Mark on the side of the head, making his ears ring, sending him off his balance. Consequently he ran into a powerful straight left, which took him in the neck. He gulped, seemed to stop breathing, swayed to one side and then fetched up against the wall, gasping for breath, and feeling the pain sear through his head and his neck.

The man with the limp rushed along the hall, and closed the door from the inside. Mark was vaguely aware of that as he tried to keep his balance. He was supporting himself weakly when the man with the limp returned and gripped his forearm.

'Keep your mouth shut,' he said abruptly.

'Er,' muttered Mark.

He was beginning to think, and what he thought was not pleasant. Roger, in an oblique fashion, and Chatsworth much more directly, had warned him what to expect of the 'other side' and he was completely in this man's hands. If he were as dangerous as reports made out, the prospect was bleak. Mark felt less frightened than confused as the other led him into the dining room.

The curtains were drawn, and the room was in darkness until the other switched on the light. Mark blinked; there were tears of pain in his eyes, and his neck felt swollen, although he was becoming more normal and able to appraise the other more detachedly. There was no indication that the man proposed to do more violence then.

'Sit down,' he said, and pushed Mark into an easy chair.

Mark sat.

'You're Mark Lessing?'

'Yes,' agreed Mark, relieved that the partly imaginary swelling in his throat did not make talking too difficult.

'A friend of West,' the man continued.

'More or less.'

'Don't waste words!' the other said. 'I haven't time for it. Listen to me, Lessing. West's got something that I want, and I am going to get it.'

'Oh,' said Mark.

'I'm going to get it,' repeated the other, and something in his expression as well as the tone of his voice made it clear that he would allow nothing to prevent him from getting what he wanted: there was an air of utter ruthlessness about him.

The man said abruptly: 'Where is West?'

'I don't know.'

'Don't lie to me. Where is he?'

'There was some talk of him going to a nursing home,' said

Mark, giving the impression that he was a little apprehensive because he could not answer the other's question. 'It's no use looking at me like that. I don't know where he is, I tell you.'

'Listen to me,' said the man with the limp, leaning forward and stroking the length of rubber with an almost feline gesture. 'No one can lie to Count Riordon and get away with it. Do you understand? I know you can tell me where West is, and before I leave here I'm going to have his address. He's gone to the country, and probably the West Country.'

'Then you know more than I do,' said Mark. 'I don't see why you shouldn't tell me where he's gone.'

'But for a little misfortune, I could have done,' said the man who called himself Count Riordon. 'He was followed as far as Salisbury, and then lost.'

'Salisbury?' Mark sounded startled. 'But that's—'

'Come on, come on,' said Riordon. 'No more lying or evading the issue. Where is West?'

It did not occur to Mark to tell him, but he experienced an unfamiliar sensation. He was afraid of the man with the limp, afraid of the way the other caressed the rubber truncheon, of the unnatural glitter in his light grey eyes. He did not try to hide it from himself. This was real, old-fashioned wind-up. Yet it was surely an absurd notion, for he himself was fairly well recovered, and, even if not quite a match physically, stood at least one chance in three of winning in a struggle. He tensed his muscles, prepared for an attack, but none materialised, although Riordon's eyes seemed to grow larger.

'Out with it.'

'I don't know,' repeated Mark. 'And I really wouldn't tell you if I did.'

He rose from his chair as he spoke, and thrust his hand into his pocket. He was prepared to follow the movement up and launch an attack if the other showed himself to be taken by surprise. But Riordon simply eased himself forward in his chair and stretched out his right leg, kicking Mark's right knee. The toecap of his shoe struck home. Mark winced, and dropped back.

Apart from anything else, including the pain, he was alarmed by the ridiculous ease with which Riordon had stopped him. His fear, which was very real, increased. He wondered what would happen if the man began to torture him, then dismissed the thought, comforting himself with the hope that Riordon could not overpower him completely enough.

'Don't be a fool,' Riordon said dispassionately. 'You aren't hurt yet, but you will be if you try any more tricks. I'll give you another chance. Where is West?'

Mark drew a deep breath. 'Somewhere in England,' he said.

Riordon rose to his feet, looking very tall; he gave the impression that he had grown appreciably in size during the past few seconds. The peculiar sense of imagery, almost of hallucination, had never been stronger. Riordon had a nightmarish effect on him, and he felt that his muscles would not respond to whatever efforts he tried to make.

'I'm a very rich man,' Riordon said abruptly.

For a moment Mark stared at him, surprised and absurdly relieved. 'Indeed?'

'A *very* rich man,' repeated Riordon. 'I am the only man in this country who has made enormous profits out of breaking the law, while remaining in a position to snap his fingers at it. The law,' he repeated with a scorn which seemed as genuine as it was well-expressed. 'A fig for the law! It cannot contain me, it cannot prevent me from doing what I like. The police know it. They *dare not* arrest me, Lessing. You thought they should have hurried after me today, didn't you? Well, so they should, and so they would have done if I had been an ordinary criminal! They know better – there is no one quite like me, and I doubt whether there will be again. You take my word for it, the police will never arrest me. I have them just where I want them, and they know it.'

The words should create an impression of a man with an overweening vanity, speaking in a wild spirit of bravado or else that the man was insane enough to believe what he said. In fact it was difficult to disbelieve him. Riordon believed they were true, and uttered them with such conviction that Mark was almost convinced. That might have had something to do with the fact that the policeman in Queen's Street had certainly shown no inclination to make an early start on chasing Riordon.

'Nonsense,' Mark made himself say.

He experienced another queer spasm: the word was uttered to answer his own thoughts, but he saw its effect on Riordon, and knew that the man believed that it was an answer to what he had said. Riordon crouched forward a little, his hands bunched; the rubber truncheon seemed absurdly small and almost enveloped in one vast palm. His lips parted a little, but his teeth did not show.

'Non-*sense*,' he echoed. '*No one* talks to me like that without apologising, *or* suffering for it.'

Mark found the words coming against his will. 'I—I'm sorry.'

'That's better.' Riordon relaxed. 'You really must be more careful how you deal with me. I am no ordinary man. If I were, the police would have had me in prison a long time ago. They are afraid of me, just as you are. The only difference is that they know me better, and are not so careless as you. I am overlooking your mistakes because I know you are so ignorant. Now I told you that I was a rich man.'

'Yes.'

'Are *you?*'

'Not what you'd call rich,' said Mark. 'I'm comfortably off, and have a fair salary, but—'

'Salary!' exclaimed Riordon. 'Only fools work for a salary. But you cannot help being what you are, can you?' He gave the sneer time to sink in. 'What would you say at the prospect of ten thousand pounds a year for life? Don't answer too quickly, give yourself time to think about it. Ten thousand pounds a year, for *life*. Two hundred pounds every week of the year. Not a miserly pension, I think you will agree.'

'P-pension!' stammered Mark.

'That is right. A pension. I should require nothing beyond the services you can render me in the next few days, and, provided your help is reliable, I will allow you the pension whether I succeed or fail in my primary object. Ten thousand pounds a year, *for the rest of your life.*'

Then suddenly: 'Where is West?' He raised a clenched hand. 'Don't tell me you have no idea. I will not believe it. I won't believe it! I will smash your body to pieces if you lie to me again. *Where is West?*'

Mark needed time, desperately – and there was one possible way to get it: by making Riordon believe that he could be bought.

'How do I know you'll pay?' he asked softly.

'I always keep my word, Lessing. No one has ever known me cheat. That kind of dishonesty is worth no one's time and trouble. How do you think I have built up my reputation without a strict observance of contracts? My word,' continued Riordon with absurd solemnity, '*is* my bond.'

'You're the most remarkable man I've ever met!' said Mark. 'Astonishing. You really are!'

Through the other's words he had caught a glimpse of incredible vanity, the monstrous confidence in himself which had led up to a conviction that he was supreme. A vain man liked nothing better than to talk about himself, and receive praise. True, there was an element of the unpredictable about this man, but the general rule might work, and he, Mark, badly needed to gain time. Until then he had been overpowered by the other's peculiar influence – it was almost hypnotic. But gradually he believed that he was getting back to normal.

'That's very discerning of you,' Riordon said at last. 'Of course, I cannot help the gifts with which I have been endowed. Every now and again a man is born who *is* outstanding. I am one. If people would only accept that as an accomplished fact, and act accordingly, life would be so much simpler. I am now gradually establishing my ascendancy over others, but I have to cope with a great deal of opposition, and prejudice is everywhere.

However, there are some, like yourself, whose eyes are opened quickly, and who do not hesitate to pay homage. Lessing, I think you might prove very useful to me, very useful indeed. Forget my talk of trifles! *If* you come successfully through your first trial, then I can use you as one of my chief stewards. Money—' he waved a hand grandiloquently. 'You need not think about it, you will have as much as you wish, for whatever purpose you wish. And after all, money buys *everything*. You are a bachelor, are you not? Very wise, sir. So am I. But I will agree that there are times when a little womanly company is welcome, even desirable. And I number some of the most beautiful women in the world amongst my companions, who will do my bidding and give pleasure to my friends at my behest. I ask nothing from them but service, and they are prepared to give me everything. Are you beginning to understand?'

Mark brushed his hand across his forehead. The night was warm, but did not account for the beads of perspiration on his forehead. 'Only—only just beginning.'

'You cannot expect to grasp so great a project swiftly,' said Riordon. 'But I think you are gifted enough to assimilate it in a comparatively short time. Now, let us be finished with preliminaries, so that I can begin to initiate you. Where did you say West is?'

'He's gone to Taunton,' lied Mark.

'Taunton? In Somerset? What address?'

'It's a village just outside.' Mark put his hand to his inside coat pocket. 'Grayling, or something like that, I've got it written down.' He took out his wallet, and Riordon rose and joined him, standing by his side and breathing very softly. Mark fought against the insidious influence of the man's proximity, and began to sort through some papers in his wallet. 'I put it in here somewhere,' he added, and then dropped the wallet. 'Oh, damn!'

He bent down.

Riordon remained standing. Several visiting cards fell from

the case, and Mark began to pick them up, glancing at each one in turn. 'No, it's not here,' he said as if to himself, and straightened up.

Riordon was standing a yard away from him, with his hands by his side, although he was frowning with displeasure at the delay. Mark had no doubt at all that he believed he had won the first round, and was going to get Roger's address.

Mark closed his fist, and drove it with all his strength towards Riordon's stomach. The blow landed before Riordon realised what was about to happen, and the man had no chance at all of backing away, or dodging it. There was a split second in which Mark felt a surge of exultation at taking the man completely off his guard, a moment of rare triumph.

Through Mark's knuckle, his hand, and his wrist, there shot a pain so excruciating that he uttered a high, involuntary cry. The pain was so great that he did not even realise that he had been outwitted, did not even grasp the fact that beneath his shirt Riordon wore either a chain waistcoat or a steel belt. Mark staggered back, holding his right arm upwards, the blood gone from his cheeks and even his lips. He could not think because of the agony, he did not even notice the cold malignance which spread over Riordon's features for his eyes were filmed with tears.

He did hear the man say something, but could not distinguish the words.

'So you thought you could deceive me,' said Riordon softly. 'You think that hurts, do you? I will teach you the meaning of pain.'

Mark Begins a Journey

'I WILL TEACH you the meaning of pain,' said Riordon again. Mark backed away, knocked against a chair and staggered. He could not put out a hand to save himself from falling, and dropped awkwardly into the chair. All the time Riordon approached him, slowly, and without once looking away from him.

There were humming and droning sounds in his ears, part of the illusion which the whole sickening episode had created; but through it there was another note, more musical. It was a tune, the air went in and out of his mind. Vaguely he thought of the radio next door. *Next door.* If only he could make a noise, even a high-pitched cry, it might bring help: he had never been so desperately in need of help.

Then Riordon looked away from him.

The man did not look startled or surprised, but his attention was momentarily diverted, and in the precious seconds which ensued Mark tried to pull himself together. Riordon had protected his stomach, but could not protect his head. 'If I could find some kind of a weapon,' Mark thought desperately. 'I might—'

Softly, surely too softly to be from the neighbour's radio, came the strains of an old, once familiar tune: Addinsell's *Warsaw Concerto*. Mark did not know what instrument was being played; the air was unmistakable, but it lacked the volume and much of the power of the theme. It was coming from the open door leading to the passage. It grew louder, and

Riordon stepped towards the door and looked out.

Mark snatched up a flower vase; some water spilled over on his hand, and several of the flowers fell as he raised the vase for throwing.

Another sound came from the passage. Mark fancied that there was a series of footsteps, and then was quite sure that a key grated in the lock. In fresh alarm, he thought: 'Janet's come back! She mustn't come in!'

Then Riordon turned and looked towards him, a sneer on his lips. He glanced at the vase, but ignored it.

'I'll settle with you later,' he said, and stepped into the hall.

Mark stepped forward and pulled the curtains aside. In front of him was the loggia where he had had tea with Roger and Janet only two days before. It was almost dark, but he caught a glimpse of a man moving at the far end of the garden.

Another man's voice spoke from behind him. 'Be careful, Mr Lessing, be careful!'

On the words, the light went out.

For once a voice coming unexpectedly did not alarm Mark, who recognised the voice of Detective Sergeant Sloan.

He did not spend time in wondering how Sloan had managed to obtain a key to the house, but swallowed hard, backed towards a chair which he knew was near, and dropped into it. He breathed heavily, ignoring Sloan but hearing the big detective step towards the window. He saw his shadow as he drew near. Sloan passed him and drew the curtains. In the utter blackness which descended upon the room, Sloan made his way cautiously to the door and switched on the light.

Mark put his hand up to shade his eyes from the glare.

He saw Sloan frown as he stared towards him, then saw the big man nod as if seeing just what he expected. He did not feel capable of speaking, cared nothing when Sloan turned from the room and went out. Mark heard sounds and imagined that among them was running water. He did not care what there was nor what happened. He was sick with pain and reaction from fright, and realised both of these things. It was useless to pretend otherwise; Riordon had frightened the wits out of him, and the effect of the man's utterances still lingered, although presumably he was some distance away by now.

Sloan returned with a bowl of water, a towel, a sponge, and a small first aid case. He did not speak, but put the bowl of water on an occasional table and began to soak a sponge in it. He wiped Mark's forehead and cheeks, then asked him if he was thirsty. Mark said that he was and was given a few sips of water. They refreshed him surprisingly, and he began to feel much better as Sloan bathed his lacerated knuckles. The swollen flesh of his right hand was already turning colour, and it was difficult to move the fingers.

'Lucky that wasn't your eye, Mr Lessing,' said Sloan, in an effort to be jocular. 'What did he hit you with?'

Mark swallowed hard. 'He didn't – I hit him.'

'*Did* you!' exclaimed Sloan, his voice reflecting genuine surprise. 'It isn't often he lets anyone start first, so you've started a precedent! No, that's the wrong verb, isn't it? *Created* a precedent, that's better. Take it easy, now, there's no hurry. He won't come back tonight, I promise you that.'

'How – can you?' Mark managed to ask.

'Because he's been warned that it will be dangerous,' said Sloan. 'Our chaps are surrounding the house now, and he never asks for trouble – not much, anyhow. You know, I think you ought to see a doctor about that hand. It doesn't look very good to me. Does it hurt?'

'Like blazes,' said Mark.

'You *might* have damaged the bone,' said Sloan pessimistically. 'What with you and the Inspector *hors de combat* in two days, that's not bad going. Feeling better? I'll make a cup of tea, shall I, and then phone a doctor. You wouldn't happen to know the address of the nearest one, would you?'

'There's a Dr Littlejohn, somewhere across the road,' said Mark. He stood up unsteadily and ran his left hand across his forehead, while Sloan bustled out of the dining room.

Sloan, who knew the house from several calls he had made

on Roger, walked along the passage; a moment or two later the ting! of the telephone bell sounded. There followed a brief conversation before the ting! came again and Sloan went to the kitchen. Soon he entered the dining room with a tray.

'A cup of tea is just what the doctor ordered – oh, that reminds me, he promised to come over in ten minutes. He'll soon put you right.' Sloan poured tea, and when Mark said that he did not take sugar, told him that this was one of the times when he was going to break the rule. The tea was hot, strong, and very sweet.

'We've been watching the house, and knew Riordon was here,' Sloan said. 'We've got a job on with him, Mr Lessing. He's in the middle of some game we don't know much about, but if we play our cards right, he'll lead us to the heart of it. That's as much as I'm allowed to tell you. Did you hear anything just before I came in?'

'Yes,' said Mark. 'Someone seemed to be playing the *Warsaw Concerto*.'

'I *thought* so,' said Sloan very slowly. 'I was pretty sure before, but now I know. The *Warsaw Concerto*. That's Riordon's signature tune, when he hears it he moves off pretty quickly. You didn't happen to see who played it, did you?'

'No,' said Mark, oddly affected by the intensity of Sloan's words. 'It came from the kitchen I think.'

'No one ever sees who plays it,' said Sloan. 'That's one of the things that we've got to try to find out. As a matter of fact I'm not sure whether it's important or whether it's just part of a scheme to put us all on edge. He's not nice to know, is he?'

'I've known people I'd rather spend an evening with,' admitted Mark.

Sloan grinned. 'Do you know, Mr Lessing, you must be better or you wouldn't be able to talk like that! Not everyone can throw off the effect of Riordon so quickly, I don't mind telling you. I've known girls be hysterical on and off for weeks.'

'Are you serious?'

'I've never been more so. That man's *evil*, Mr Lessing.' There was a ring at the front door. 'Ah, here's the doctor, I think. While he's looking at your hand, Mr Lessing, I'll telephone the Yard. You don't mind?'

A moment later he ushered Dr Littlejohn into the room.

Mark knew the portly, bustling doctor slightly, having played bridge with him, Roger and Janet. A greyhead with bright blue eyes and a bluff, rather abrupt manner, Littlejohn raised his bushy eyebrows when he saw Mark, and said: 'Now what have you been up to?'

'Hitting my hand against a brick wall,' said Mark, which was as near the truth as he proposed going with the doctor. Sloan went out and Littlejohn advanced, putting a small bag on a chair. He frowned when he looked at the hand, pursed his lips and exuded several short breaths, with a peculiar whistling note, like an asthmatic patient.

He busied himself with lint, bandages, and ointment, all taken from his bag: the ointment was soothing, cool and pleasant. Nevertheless the dressing was painful, and took nearly ten minutes. When it was finished the whole of Mark's right hand was bandaged, and looked, he said, like a white-coated ham.

Littlejohn went off, and when he had gone Sloan entered the dining room again.

'He won't be long,' he said.

'Who?' asked Mark, surprised.

'Sir Guy. He's given orders to be told about everything to do with Riordon. I explained a little to his highness, and he said he would come right over. I'll leave you now, sir.'

Sloan went out.

There was a ring at the front door bell, and Mark walked along to answer it, reflecting that he would have a very different angle to discuss with Chatsworth this time. Two plain-clothes men on the drive were visible against the lights of a car which stood beyond the burly figure of Sir Guy. He nodded as he entered the hall and waited until Mark closed the door before he spoke. Then it was gruffly. 'So you won't take a friendly warning, Lessing?'

'We don't mean the same thing by the word friendly,' Mark retorted.

'Possibly not. What happened to your hand?'

'I proved that Riordon's stomach is made of iron,' said Mark sardonically.

'So you managed to get at close quarters, did you?' Chatsworth seemed surprised. 'You should have taken my advice. I couldn't have warned you any more clearly, and I don't *want* to have to detain you even for your own 'This time even you would come unstuck if you tried,' said Mark. 'This house is where I live. The Wests have let me have a couple of rooms until I find another flat. I have every right to be here and to sleep here, whether the Wests are at home or not. Does that make any impression on you?'

Chatsworth looked shaken.

'I didn't know that.'

'Then perhaps we've a basis for discussion,' said Mark. 'I came here to sleep. When I opened the door a man who called himself Count Riordon was standing on the stairs. There was nothing I could do about it, even if I'd wanted to. I closed with him. He got the better of the first scuffle – and the last, for that matter. But I suppose you would like the detailed story?'

'Please,' said Chatsworth, much more mildly.

'The first thing is that I don't really believe in Riordon,' Mark said. 'I saw him, hit him, struggled with him and was scared out of my wits by him, but now he's gone I don't really believe any of it.'

'I know exactly what you mean,' Chatsworth said.

Mark found the telling easier than he had anticipated. He told the story simply, without laying undue emphasis on any point in it, except Riordon's confidence that the police dared not arrest him. He talked of the grandiloquence of the bribe, or 'pension', and Riordon's eager acceptance of and reaction to effusive praise.

When he had finished, he took a cigarette case from his

pocket and tried to light the cigarette one-handed. Chatsworth appeared so absorbed in the story that he let Mark struggle before saying suddenly: 'All right, I'll do that.' He struck a match, and as Mark drew in a breath of smoke, he added: 'So now you've met Count Riordon.'

'Is he really a Count?'

'Oh yes,' said Chatsworth airily. 'Obscure Italian antecedents, I understand. Born in Ireland, two generations removed from his nearest Italian relatives, but some of the family died very quickly and Riordon inherited. It's no more than a title, but he has every right to it.'

'Did he get his money from the same source?' asked Mark heavily.

'No.' Chatsworth brushed a hand over the smooth patch of his cranium, and leaned back in an easy chair. 'No,' he repeated. 'He did not inherit his money. I think he stole it.'

Mark stared. 'Really rich on ill-gotten gains?'

'We don't know what he's worth,' said Chatsworth, 'but it wouldn't surprise us if he has something in common with Croesus. Yes, Riordon's got plenty of money. I don't propose to tell you the whole story, Lessing, but if you're in Riordon's black books you may as well be told sooner or later. West can tell you. And as you know Riordon, you'd better have your own way, and try to help us – if you still want to.'

His expression suggested that he half-expected Mark to decide that discretion was the better part of valour. And Mark hesitated. He was ashamed of his own hesitation, yet could not free his mind of the horror of Riordon. *'I'll teach you the meaning of pain,'* Riordon had said.

Mark shivered.

'Well?' asked Chatsworth.

Mark said slowly: 'Of course I want to. Tell me – is there any truth in Riordon's statement that the police are afraid to arrest him? That seems to be the crux of the matter.'

'There are no grounds for saying that the police are *afraid* to arrest Riordon, but there is some justification for saying that, at the moment, it is not in the national interests to do so. We have to hold our hand. Had we really wished to, we would have picked up Riordon some time ago. We have been compelled to allow him considerable rope, because – well, West can tell you that, too,' added Chatsworth grimly. 'But before you decide anything definitely, Lessing, think again. You've met the man now, and you know what the affair might lead to.'

The Village of Hinton Magna

'I'M CERTAINLY in this,' Mark said. 'I don't know that it would be a lot of good if I tried to keep out. Riordon didn't give me the impression of making threats in vain.'

'He wouldn't,' said Chatsworth. 'That's right as far as it goes. If you care to stand aside, say so. If you're coming in, don't make it half-hearted.'

'I'm not half-hearted,' said Mark grimly.

'Good, good. Well, I'll leave you now. You can travel down to Hinton Magna tomorrow, and I'll send word to West that he can confide in you. Stay there with him for a few days, until you can use that hand again. What about your own work?'

'I can take some leave,' Mark said.

'Lucky man. I won't say I'm sorry that it's worked out this way, but I will say that you'll probably regret it. Still, it's your own decision. What are you going to do tonight?'

'Go to bed,' answered Mark. 'Er – can Sloan talk to me?'

'Yes, yes,' answered Chatsworth, testily.

In the hall the AC exchanged a word with Sloan. Several plain-clothes men were about, all shadowy figures in the starlit gloom. Sloan said little until they were alone in the living room. Then: 'I'm surprised he's let you in on this, Mr Lessing. You wouldn't have been if you hadn't come across Riordon. So he scared you?'

'Wouldn't he scare you?'

'I've known men I've liked better,' said Sloan. 'But he's not so almighty as he makes out. He pretends that he can snap his fingers at us, but he sheers off pretty quick when we're about. He's—' Sloan paused, searching for the right word, and went on with a harsh note: 'Uncanny, Mr Lessing, that's the word. He always seems to know when we are away for a little while. Like tonight. We'd been watching the house for some time, although we haven't always shown ourselves. Riordon didn't come near. As Roger and Janet are away our men were taken off for the first time for weeks – and Riordon turned up! It's uncanny, there's no other word for it.'

'Yes.' Mark knew just what Old Bill Sloan meant. 'What brought you back?'

'One of the local plain-clothes men knew Riordon, and happened to see him coming this way,' said Sloan. 'He reported it, and Sir Guy asked me to come. He told me to see what I could do, and sent four other men to surround the place. The thing is, Riordon can't be detained yet, but Sir Guy keeps harassing him. It's the only way. Well, I arrived, and I had a key – the Inspector gave me one some time ago. I knew Riordon was inside, and I had an idea of what might be happening to you so I decided to stop it. But I don't know that I would have succeeded, Mr Lessing, if I hadn't heard that tune. The *Warsaw Concerto.*' Sloan pronounced it 'consairto'. 'It's a kind of warning for Riordon, because whenever he hears it the police – or danger of some kind – are near. Now I ask you, *how* does he manage it? And *who* plays the blasted tune? *I've* never seen anybody, but I've heard it when I've been ahead of our chaps somewhere near Riordon. Sometimes I think I'm crazy, and it was a long time before the bosses believed me. But Roger heard it once and after that there wasn't any argument. Do you know what it's played on?'

'No.'

'A mouth organ,' declared Sloan. 'A harmonica, that's what! The son-of-a-gun knows how to play the thing, doesn't he? It's uncanny, too. I wish I hadn't landed the Riordon job, and I don't mind admitting it.'

'You don't happen to know why the police can't take him, do

you?'

Sloan said: 'No, sir, I don't.'

Mark was quite sure that he would get nothing more out of the detective sergeant. He went to sleep with the tune running through his head – although he hadn't expected to sleep at all.

Janet West, sitting in a deckchair under the shade of an apple tree on which the fruit was already beginning to form, looked at Roger and frowned ruefully. In a bath chair, which her cousin Paula had borrowed from a neighbour, he was tucked up in blankets and leaning back with his mouth slightly open and his eyes closed.

He was asleep.

Janet was darning a pair of his socks.

From the kitchen, which overlooked the small orchard of Hinton Cottage, there came sounds of running water, humming voices, and an occasional explosive comment, usually when Paula Dean put something where she should not have done or failed to find it where it should be. Paula had a girl of fifteen in the house to help her, and had refused to let Janet do more than make the bed in their own room, and use a duster. Judging from her appearance, Paula had said forthrightly, she needed a rest just as much as Roger.

The trees in the village were in full leaf. There was a majestic chestnut in the village square that towered above the oaks and beech, over the cottages, the grey square Norman church, the Manor House, and Hinton Farm. The cottage was at one end of the village, standing back from the second-class road which connected it with the main Dorchester-Blandford road some three miles away.

Hinton Magna, set in a shallow, hill-clad valley, was more sleepy even than most Dorset villages, and Janet, who knew several of them, liked its restfulness as much as the picturesque appearance of the cottages, the square green, and the chestnut trees.

Looking upwards through a tracery of foliage and branches,

Janet saw the perfect blue of the cloudless sky. The sun was shining through some gaps between the leaves, sending a gentle light over Roger, although the trees gave enough shadow to prevent him from getting too hot. Yet when she moved she realised how hot it was.

A man strolled past the cottage; she could just see his head and shoulders. He was heavily built, a man who had travelled down from London by car in the wake of the ambulance, and with two other men he shared the task of watching Paula Dean's home. Janet wished that were not considered necessary. She shied from wondering why, just as she shied from wondering why Mark Lessing had not arrived. She had felt quite sure that he would come down the previous afternoon.

Then she heard the telephone.

Paula appeared at a bedroom window with a dustcap over her bright auburn hair, the sun glinting on a few wisps which escaped the cap, and showing up her shiny nose and bright red cheeks.

'Tele-*phone!*' she shouted, and shook a duster out of the window. 'Darling, are you asleep too?'

Janet, already heading for the cottage, shook her fist, and went inside. The telephone was in the hall, a low-ceilinged, raftered place of charm, with brasses and copper glistening as the sun found a way through the leaded panes of the lattice windows. There was a small, comfortable tapestry-covered stool by the side of the old-fashioned candlestick type telephone.

It was just after twelve o'clock.

'That wouldn't be Mrs Janet West, would it?' demanded Mark.

'Mark, where have you been? Why didn't you come yesterday?'

'I have been making up my mind,' replied Mark with dignity. 'It took a great deal of doing. Have you discovered whether Paula wants me to hand out the prizes at a Guides' whist-drive, or give a speech at a garden party? Because if she does—'

'I think you'll be safe this time,' Janet said, 'except—' she paused. 'Paula thinks you ought to meet a friend who's staying at the Manor,' said Janet. 'I promised not to warn you, but—'

Mark groaned. 'Feminine gender, I take it? Long in the tooth and full of worldly wisdom, a disappointed woman who will remain forever a spinster, although Paula will doubtless want to wish her on to me? All of that?'

'And worse,' said Janet feelingly. 'But don't tell her that I've warned you.'

'You've probably hatched this story up to harass me on the journey,' declared Mark. 'What is the creature's name?'

'Marion.'

'Well, that could be worse. How's Roger?'

'Catching up on his sleep,' replied Janet.

'That's fine,' said Mark, and then disturbed her by adding: 'I had a minor collision with a taxicab yesterday, and didn't do my right hand any good. But all being well I'll be catching the 3.35 from Waterloo.' As if to prevent her from asking questions, he added: 'I've got to hurry, someone's ringing at the front door. Expect me when you see me.'

'Come soon!' said Janet. She replaced the receiver, looking towards the front lawn, which was just visible through the open door. As she sat there Paula appeared, poking her head over the banister rail of a staircase which twisted and turned and had oak beams at awkward places above it. Paula's dustcap was awry, and there was a mop and a duster in her hand as she rested it against the wood.

'Well, did you tell him?' she demanded eagerly.

Janet started, and looked up. 'Oh, you scared me! Er – yes, of course I told him. He's putting up his defences against Marion already. You really want to get him married off, don't you?'

'Men weren't made for a single life,' declared Paula. 'If it weren't for Jim I'd set my cap at him myself.'

'If it weren't for Jim you'd be the most miserable woman in England. He's had an accident,' she added abruptly.

Paula gripped the banister. 'You mean Jim?'

'Oh, what a fool I am. No, Mark. I wish he'd been more open

about it. He's hurt his hand, he says.'

'Oh, only his hand,' sniffed Paula. 'I was going to have something to say about having two invalids but a few fingers more or less won't matter. Be a pet and remind me to make sure that I ask Marion to lunch tomorrow, won't you? On Sunday it's a dreadful meal up at the Manor. They still keep formal. What time will Mark be here?'

'He wasn't sure.'

'That man wants *hand*ling,' declared Paula.

Janet went out into the orchard, half-expecting to find Roger awake; instead he was still sleeping, and continued to sleep until the gong went for lunch, banged vigorously by Paula.

He awakened slowly, put his head on one side, stared at Janet with an expression in his eyes which made her heart turn over.

'Roger!' she exclaimed. 'Roger, what is it?'

'Eh?' said Roger West. 'What – er, sorry, old girl. Had a dream, that's all. Heard something, didn't I?'

'A dream?' said Janet. 'A nightmare, you mean.'

She stopped abruptly.

She was scared, for she had never seen Roger looking quite so frightened, perhaps even horrified, as he had been when he had first been awakened.

Music was coming softly from the house. Janet saw Roger's head jerk back. Then his hands gripped the armrests of the chair, and she could see the whiteness of his knuckles.

'That tune,' he whispered hoarsely. 'That tune! It's—'

'The *Warsaw Concerto*,' said Janet as steadily as she could. 'On the radio, idiot. What's the matter with you?'

Roger said tensely: 'Is it the radio? Are you sure?'

Much About Riordon

IT WAS THE RADIO, and as they approached the windows the tune finished and the dispassionate voice of the announcer gave the next piece, which some little-known performer on the harmonica was about to render. Janet, pale because of the effect of the tune on Roger, said with forced lightness: 'It was a mouth organ, darling.'

'Yes,' said Roger. 'Yes, I thought it was. Sorry, sweet.' He half-turned to look up at her, and touched the back of her head. 'That dream had associations with the *Concerto,* and I don't think I'm really awake yet. But I can walk into the dining room, don't coddle me!'

He was more himself after lunch and went for a walk round the front garden, wearing only a dressing gown and slippers. Janet was hailed by an acquaintance who passed in the road and went for a gossip, while Paula was intent on some knitting. Roger went slowly and deliberately towards the far end of the garden. There, half-hidden in shrubs and against a background of hawthorn, was one of the Yard men who had been detailed to guard the cottage.

'Oh, it's you, Sloan. Good. That's a big help.'

'Hello, sir,' said Detective Sergeant 'Old Bill' Sloan, his fresh and ingenuous face showing satisfaction at the sight of Roger. 'Glad to see you about again. How are you?'

'I'm all right,' said Roger. 'Listen to me, and warn me if either my wife or Mrs Dean come this way. There was some music on the Light Programme just before one o'clock. I don't know what it was, except that there was a man who played the *Warsaw Concerto*. On a *harmonica,'* added Roger softly. 'Find out who it was, and get word to the Yard at once even if it means leaving here. Understand?'

'Roger!' Janet's voice came, clear and a little anxious. 'Roger!'

The sergeant slipped out of sight, hidden by the hedge and the trees, and Janet rounded a cypress. She saw Roger, who made a face at her.

'You fool, I thought something had happened to you!'

'And why should it, right here and now?' demanded Roger. 'Where's Paula?' He put an arm round Janet's waist, glanced round with mock apprehension, and added: 'As she's not in sight, you're going to be kissed.'

'You're *much* better,' said Janet breathlessly, some minutes later.

Roger's spirits remained at their new high. He successfully led Paula into believing that he was not only much better in himself, but was thoroughly enjoying the rest. There were moments when he almost convinced Janet; had she not seen his expression when he had awakened, and his tension when he had heard the *Warsaw Concerto,* she might have been fooled. Certainly nothing else happened to disturb the serenity of Hinton Magna.

Roger and Janet were on the porch when Lessing arrived. Dusk was beginning to cast its shadows, and the birds were settling down noisily. The sound of faint organ music came from the church, where the organist was practising the anthem for the morning service. There was no sign of Sloan or any of the other policemen.

There was little prospect of talking quietly to Roger that evening, but one or two leading questions in the few minutes that they did contrive to have alone made it obvious that Roger had not yet received Chatsworth's permission to talk freely.

All of the party were in bed soon after eleven o'clock.

The peacefulness of Hinton Magna and the starlit beauty of the night, even the occasional hooting of an owl, made it easy to relax. For two days they did little else. Sloan called to see Roger once a day, and also handed him a typewritten message from Chatsworth, telling him that he could pass on all he knew to Mark and giving him a résumé of what Mark had been doing.

That was on Monday.

On the Sunday there had been a considerable disappointment for Paula: relatives descended upon the Byrne family at the Manor, and Marion Byrne was unable to get away, even for half an hour. Mark affected enormous relief, and called it fate. The day passed pleasantly, with little or no undercurrent, except Mark's misgivings about the sincerity of Chatsworth's promise. They were dispersed early on the Monday morning, soon after Sloan's visit.

Roger, dressed in slacks and a tweed jacket for the first time since his convalescence had started, disarmingly suggested that he and Mark would be in the way at the cottage, and proposed a stroll to the village to replenish Mark's stock of cigarettes and his own of tobacco.

They did in fact call at the village shop for cigarettes, and then they went towards the Manor grounds, and there, in a clearing surrounded by saplings and shrubs, where the grass was cropped short by rabbits, they sat down and lit their pipes.

On the way to the village Roger had told Mark of Chatsworth's message, and so there was no need for preliminaries.

Roger smiled a little reminiscently, patted his adhesive plaster, and looked at Mark's hand. 'The marks of the beast,' he said, almost flippantly. 'I wanted to keep you out of this show.'

'That was a friendly thought,' agreed Mark with a grimace. 'The thing that I can't grasp is why Riordon's still at liberty. I don't doubt there's a pretty good reason, but I'm damned if I can see a glimpse of it. He *is* dangerous, isn't he?'

'Let's stop talking in clichés,' said Roger. 'Dangerous isn't the word. He's deadly. I haven't yet made up my mind whether he's insane or not. Mark, you're going to have a shock in a few minutes.'

'I'll try to take it.'

There was a queer expression in Roger's eyes; it was as if he were looking at something a long distance off.

'I've known Riordon now for about six months, but he has been active a great deal longer than that,' he said. 'He specialised in confidence tricks and blackmail, the two varieties of crime which, given victims of some standing, are likely to remain undetected. I've talked to several of Riordon's early victims, and they all say the same. He didn't drive them too far. As far as they could be, in such a business, they were satisfied. They had a shock when I turned up and started questioning them.'

'How did you learn their names?' inquired Mark.

'One of the victims wanted to get his own back but was anxious to avoid the publicity of police action. So he hired Pep Morgan.' Morgan was a private inquiry agent. 'Morgan, having no idea of what he was up against, took the case on. Riordon was, and is, so filled with conceit that in the early days he did not take ordinary precautions, and Morgan managed to get hold of a notebook which had the names of the victims and the amounts they had paid. There were no details, just the names and addresses. Then something broke, and Morgan had an "interview" with Riordon. Morgan came to tell us about it, without mentioning his original client, of course.

'Then the wife of a permanent official at Whitehall disappeared. She was fifteen years younger than her husband, and was known to have *affaires*. We found her in a cottage hospital in Surrey. One of the nurses had seen her photograph in a weekly paper, and remarked on the likeness. Riordon had kidnapped her, and fed her with drugs. I won't mention her name,' said Roger, and for the first time tension fell upon him, a bleakness showed in his face. 'She had arrived at the hospital dressed in rags, suffering from exhaustion, and giving no name. She was very nearly insane, and in fact is still undergoing treatment. Now and again she mentions one name – Riordon's. The medical and nursing staff all agreed that it terrified her.'

Mark's mouth was dry.

'She hasn't yet told us anything else that happened to her,' continued Roger, 'but we had a sudden crop of similar cases – disappearances, usually of youngish and good-looking women who eventually turned up suffering from drugs, loss of memory, a complete nervous breakdown. Most of them mentioned the dreaded name. In many cases they were wives of highly placed Government officers, in others the wives of young senior officers in the services, particularly Air Force men. How they made contact with Riordon we don't yet know. None of them will talk freely, either because they can't or they daren't. Can you see the picture forming?' Roger added quietly.

'It's not nice,' said Mark. His voice seemed to choke him.

'Nice! It's the very heart of evil! Mind you, at first we didn't think a great deal of it. We took it for granted that Riordon used drugs. There were indications that he dabbled in black magic, too, and there are always a few sensation seeking women who will do anything for kicks. But some of the people involved weren't the type, and that was puzzling. Well, we assumed that we had only to catch Riordon and put him under lock and key, to make him break down. We knew he must have some infamous establishment somewhere, and kept searching for it, while we had his description from Pep Morgan and the earlier victims. All the time, of course, it was wise to keep the business secret.'

He paused, then added slowly: 'It wasn't a question of hush-hush for the sake of the reputation of high Government officials. There might have been a case for that alone, but there was much more to it. The commander of a submarine, say, suddenly discovered that his wife was not at home, that she stopped corresponding, and that her friends and relatives had no news of her. Delegates at Disarmament Conferences learned that their wives were missing. Nuclear physicists doing secret work suffered, too. For each one it was bad enough to create for the husband a particular hell of his own. But supposing the Riordon story was released? Supposing that each husband knew that his wife was one of many, and that most of the others had come back physically and mentally wrecked. You begin to see?'

Mark said thinly: 'A problem. Yes.'

'For better or worse it was decided on the strength of that to keep everything quiet and to go for Riordon by stealth. Once we had him, we thought, it would be reasonably safe to let the story break, but while he was at large it couldn't be done. Chatsworth saw the Home Secretary before making any decision, of course, and I believe it was discussed by the Cabinet. The hush-hush policy wasn't ours alone, you see, although we recommended it. Chatsworth decided to warn off anyone who tried to horn in from the outside, and you were one of his especial concerns – as well as one of mine! It was inevitable that sooner or later you would see that something unusual was brewing, and you wouldn't have been yourself if you hadn't wanted to take part in it. So Chatsworth decided to warn you, if you did show interest, and to follow it up with a brief spell in the lock-up if you persisted.'

'H'm,' said Mark. 'It might have been justifiable, but did he really have authority?'

'Oh yes,' said Roger, and screwed up his eyes. 'You've only heard part of it yet. Riordon was pretty catholic in his choice of victims and chose the daughter of one of our top nuclear men. We'll call him Smith. Smith relied a great deal on his daughter, and when she disappeared he began to search for her, especially as the police appeared to take little interest in the case. I don't know who saw Smith when he first reported it, but whoever it was made a hash of the business. Smith should have been reassured enough to send him back reasonably happily to work. He wasn't, so he began to look for his daughter himself.

'The odd thing is that he found her and she was all right,' continued Roger slowly. 'She'd been scared, but no more. She wouldn't tell him exactly what had happened, though. He settled down again, while she went on normally, until—' again Roger paused, and was quiet for a long time, before repeating: 'Until he heard from Riordon, who wanted five thousand pounds. If he didn't get it, he said, he would take the daughter away again. Smith came tearing round to the Yard, and I saw him myself. Chatsworth did, too. We told him as much as we thought was safe. We wanted Riordon as soon as we could – that was about two months ago – and we still thought that we had only to catch him to stop his little game. He had slipped through our fingers twice, and usually had been warned of our coming by the mouth organ rendering of the *Warsaw Concerto*. A fantastic touch,' said Roger with a crooked smile, 'but only one of such touches. However, Riordon realised that our attentions were getting dangerous, and for the first time made us realise what kind of a man and what kind of job we were up against.'

'Well?' asked Mark after a long pause.

'He kidnapped both Smith and the daughter,' said Roger simply. 'After a week he sent the daughter back again with a letter. It was very short and concise. He named many people whom he had under his control and told us that if he were arrested none of them would be seen again. They included some of our most brilliant nuclear and chemical research workers. It dawned on us then that the main motive was his kidnapping of the scientists. Some of their womenfolk had been influenced by drugs, but we put that down as subsidiary. In fact they were the important factors, for the research men were persuaded to go somewhere –

I don't yet know where – to see their womenfolk. The men just disappeared. They all went on the day before Riordon named them.' Roger drew a deep breath, as if he too were fighting against belief in this horror. 'They matter, Mark. Two Harwell men, two specialists on conventional high explosives, two medical research men, some of the best brains in the country are missing.'

'It couldn't be much worse,' Mark said slowly.

'Blackmail on a vaster scale than I'd ever dreamed about,' Roger said flatly. 'There have been times when I haven't been able to believe in it, but there it is and we have to face it. Thirty or forty people are missing, one in every four a woman. Presumably they are in Riordon's power. The major problem is to find where they are. Until we know that we dare not hold Riordon, for fear he has arranged for them to die. It would be a macabre conception of the purposes of hostages, and he has said that it is just what he will do.' Roger paused, and went on slowly: 'The possibilities are frightening, but you don't need telling that. For one thing Riordon might be able to find what these people know, and could pass on vital information to Russia or China. As far as we know we've blocked any channels he might have of sending them abroad, but until we find the missing people, he has us where he wants us. Once we've found them we can go for him. Until we have, we can't. It's as simple as that. Of course,' Roger added, 'the theory of first getting Riordon, who's at the heart of the business, and so breaking up everything else, has to be considered. The trouble is that we aren't by any means sure that Riordon is in this on his own. He must have assistance, and he might have someone ready to step into his shoes if anything happens to him. Not easy, is it?'

Mark pulled a few pieces of grass from a molehill, and then said slowly: 'If I hadn't seen Riordon I don't think I would have believed it.'

'Well, you have. And now you've some idea of what the man might do. Obviously it isn't a case of orthodox police investigation methods. I've been working on it for weeks, as you know. Those night calls always came when someone else, usually a woman, had been reported missing. The morning when you followed me' – Roger smiled – 'I'd seen you, and I had an idea what Janet wanted you to do! – it was rather different. The body of one of Riordon's victims had been found in the Thames, on the other side of the Albert Bridge. She'd been seen to throw herself in the river, and there was no doubt that it was suicide. Equally there was no doubt that she had been driven to it by Riordon. Just why he decided to have a cut at me then, I don't know. Incidentally, I haven't yet thanked you for keeping me afloat,' he added abruptly.

'Don't be an ass,' said Mark uncomfortably. 'I haven't stopped cursing myself for letting them throw you in. How did you know, anyhow?'

'Sloan told me yesterday,' said Roger. 'Well, that's the position as it is now, and I don't see that we can do a great deal until we're both fit again. I wouldn't like to risk a clash with Riordon in my present state, and you' – he looked at the bandaged hand, poking from a sling – 'how did you really get that?'

'Punching Riordon.'

He went on to explain what had happened, and added: 'Which reminds me, Riordon is convinced that you've got something which could be dangerous to him, and that no one else has it. Have you? Or are you fooling him?'

Roger said thoughtfully: 'I may have it.'

'Don't you *know?*'

'I've discovered one or two little items of information,' said Roger. 'When I picked up some papers which Riordon had in his pocket one day, there was a small map amongst them. I can't remember it in detail, but I think I would be able to remember more if I saw the map again, or another of the same place. I marked the one I found, to try to be sure it wasn't slightly altered, to confuse the issue. It was quite small, and there were no names on it, but the usual little dots indicated towns or villages. I haven't any idea what part of England it's in, and can't even use the map again and get a cartographer to trace the district for me. Riordon managed to get it back.' Roger scowled. 'There are times when I think we're still underestimating him. The map was stolen when my pocket was picked on the way to the Yard.'

'If this were any other case that would be funny,' said Mark.

'Yes, wouldn't it,' Roger said drily. 'Well, there it is. Riordon may think that by seeing the map I've seen enough to be dangerous, and – what's the matter?' He broke off at a gesture from Mark.

'Now steady,' said Mark quickly. 'You're not seeing the wood for the trees. Your pocket was picked, and the wallet was stolen?'

'It was.'

'And you've assumed that Riordon did it?'

'Or one of his men, yes,' agreed Roger slowly. 'But—'

'There are times when the police are much too orthodox,' Mark told him sadly. 'He wouldn't have come to your place, he wouldn't be so desperately anxious to find you, if he didn't think you had the map. Someone *else* did that pocket-picking.'

Roger said slowly: 'It wouldn't surprise me if you're right. Why the devil hasn't someone seen that possibility before?'

He broke off again but this time it was not at an interruption from Mark. It was at a sharp cry from nearby, a cry which made Mark turn his head abruptly. It came from the thicket about them, in a woman's voice.

'Get away,' she cried. *'Get away!'*

The Reappearance of a Tramp

THERE FOLLOWED a scuffling sound, although whether it was made by the girl running, or by a struggle, neither Mark nor Roger could guess. Roger rose to his feet more swiftly than Mark, who could not put his right hand down as a lever, and forced a way through the bushes. Mark followed seconds later. Roger was the first to see the girl and the tramp.

The girl was standing by a stunted oak tree, staring at the tramp; to Roger it looked as if she had tried to get farther away, but had been stopped by the thick undergrowth. The tramp was sideways towards him, holding up a hand in a protesting, even an appealing, fashion, and whining: 'Quiet, Miss, quiet. You ain't got no reason to be scared, I promise you. Just you keep quiet.'

The girl looked beyond the tramp and caught sight of Roger. Her expression of relief was so obvious that the tramp looked round, startled. Roger saw the man's expression change, saw the cunning which crossed his countenance, allied, he judged, to alarm. In a flash the tramp, overdressed and looking very fat, moved towards a gap in the undergrowth. He cast a sidelong look at Roger as he did so.

Mark came up.

Roger's one interest was to catch the tramp before he took advantage of the trees and shrubs to disappear, but the undergrowth baulked him, and he was not fit enough to jump into the clearing. The girl straightened up, and the tramp shuffled towards safety with surprising speed.

Then Mark exclaimed: *'Parker!'*

Parker ignored the shout, and went on. Roger caught his foot in a bramble, winced as the thorns scratched his leg and staggered. He blocked Mark's path, and in any case Mark was in no better shape than Roger for following the man. Muttering under his breath, Roger freed himself from the thorns as Crummy Parker disappeared. Before Roger and Mark joined the girl the sounds of the tramp's movement had faded.

The girl watched her rescuers.

She was tall, she wore a linen frock, and her hair was very fair; those facts registered on Roger's mind as well as on Mark's. She looked pale and a little embarrassed, and the reason for that was quickly explained.

'It's all right,' she said hastily. 'He didn't do any harm. I was startled when I saw him, and thought he was going to attack me. It was silly.'

'Oh, that's all right,' said Roger, peering along the path. 'I wish we weren't half-crippled, or we'd have a word with the gentleman.'

The girl smiled. 'Yes, I suppose so. Oughtn't your arm to be in the sling?'

Mark glanced down, raised one eyebrow above the other, and readjusted the sling awkwardly. The trio stood in momentary silence.

'We can't stand here all day,' said Mark. 'Can we see you out of the woods, Miss—'

'Byrne,' said the girl when he paused.

'Byrne!' exclaimed Mark. 'Not—'

'Look here,' said Roger hastily, 'I can't help it, Mark, but I must have a word with Sloan. My mind's gone rusty. I've only just realised what Parker might do. I'll be seeing you. Er – goodbye, Miss Byrne.'

He strode off in the wake of Crummy Parker, leaving Mark regarding the girl with an ironic little smile.

'He's like that,' he said. 'Ever unpredictable. Now I'll have to escort you myself.'

They fell into step. 'As a matter of fact we ought really to know each other. But for the visitors to the Manor you would have had lunch with me yesterday.'

'Lunch with—' she began, and then her expression cleared. 'Oh, of course. You're staying with Paula Dean?'

'That's right.'

She said: *'You're* not Inspector West?'

'Oh no,' said Mark. 'I'm neither so famous nor so clever. I'm Inspector West's Watson on favoured occasions, and just a useless encumbrance at others. I stay behind to pick up the pieces – figuratively speaking! And I look after the courtesies, too.'

'You're all that Paula said you were.'

'I don't much like the sound of that. Paula isn't always charitable. So I don't have to introduce myself?'

'Not if you're Mark Lessing.'

'I'm Mark Lessing,' said Mark. A few yards farther along the path they reached the end of the thicket, where the going was much easier.

Farther away, beyond another thicket, it was possible for them to see the outlines of the top of the Manor.

'You weren't by any chance going to Paula's for lunch?' said Mark.

'I was.'

'Well, well,' said Mark. 'That shows you the advantages of taking a short cut.'

They laughed together. Then they caught sight of Roger, walking towards them quickly. He smiled as he drew near, turned and fell into step with them, walking on Marion's other side.

They reached the drive of the Manor before walking to the byroad, and then through Hinton Magna towards the cottage. There were a few people in the village streets. Marion said suddenly: 'I ought to get some darning wool here. I won't be a jiffy.'

She disappeared into a shop and the front door bell clanged

as she closed it. Mark merged a frown with a smile as he said: 'It's almost as if she knew we'd like a few minutes on our own.'

'Yes,' said Roger. 'Mark, do you see what it means?'

'I'm not dazzled by her as much as all that,' said Mark reproachfully. 'Parker was listening in.'

'He probably heard much more than we wanted,' said Roger. 'I met Sloan, and told him to get a call put out for the beggar, but it may be too late. What I want to know is how you came to recognise Parker. I've seen him several times, but he didn't spring to my mind as quickly as he did yours.'

'You haven't been told how I was put in clink,' said Mark. 'He was amongst those who watched you being thrown into the river.' Mark paused, concentration wrinkled his forehead. 'I'm beginning to wonder more and more about Crummy Parker and his remarkable prescience. I will explain that later,' he added, for the clanging of the door bell at the shop heralded Marion Byrne. 'Is there anything we can do now?'

'Sloan will do all he can, and you and I have to take it easily anyhow,' Roger said. 'The more seriously I take this rest period the quicker I can get busy.'

'Chatsworth will be told, I suppose?'

Roger nodded. Mark, he thought, was not quite himself, although his smile when he greeted Marion was characteristic. Roger walked quietly while the others talked cheerfully; he was contemplating the unpleasant implications of Parker's appearance in the grounds of the Manor.

How much had the man heard? If he now knew all that Roger had told Mark, it meant that there was a known bad character in possession of facts which might do considerable harm if put abroad, even as a rumour. Uneasily, Roger imagined Chatsworth's reaction to this misfortune.

Metaphorically shrugging his shoulders, because there was little he could do about it, he paid more attention to the banter between Mark and Marion Byrne. Then another question arose in his mind.

How was it that Marion Byrne had drawn so near without

disturbing him or Mark? They had heard nothing until her cry, yet she had been so near that ordinary progress should have been audible.

Had she been listening, too?

Conclusions

'OUGHTN'T YOU to try to have a nap, darling?' Janet suggested after lunch. 'You're looking more tired than you were before lunch.'

'If he will go about chasing tramps what do you expect?' demanded Paula. '*I* have some calls to make, and there's a jam-making session at the Women's Institute this afternoon. Are you coming, Jan? Don't if you'd rather stay here with Roger.'

'I think I'll go up to my room,' Roger said. 'Mark and Marion can look after themselves, and you two can make as much jam as you like. Don't expect me to eat it, that's all I ask!'

He grinned as he rose from his chair, and Janet accompanied him to their room at the top of the cottage.

'If you do go out you won't start anything, will you?' demanded Janet.

'Such as?' asked Roger lazily.

'More chases after tramps!'

'Only in my dreams,' he assured her lightly. 'My sweet, Sloan and the men outside will look after anything that comes along. I'm on a rest cure.'

'I can't understand why you take it so lightly,' said Janet, running a comb through her dark hair. 'I half-expected you to be on edge to get back to town as soon as you felt that you could stand up on your own. Roger, nothing's going to happen here, is it?'

She paused in the combing and stared at his reflection in the mirror, believing that he did not realise that the reflection was so clear.

'I can't be sure what's going to happen, and Chatsworth is worried or he wouldn't have sent Sloan down here. But I know of nothing impending, sweet.'

'Honestly?'

'Cross my throat,' said Roger, leaning forward and kissing the nape of her neck.

'Jan-*et!*' cried Paula from across the narrow landing. 'Are you coming?'

'Just a moment! I'm nearly ready.'

Janet finished combing, patted her hair into position and tucked some tiny pins in place, ran a powder puff lightly over her face, and stood up. She looked at Roger and was obviously waiting for comment.

'All right?' she said, when it did not come.

'Even better than usual,' Roger assured her earnestly. 'You've too much powder on the side of your nose.' He rubbed it with his finger, kissed the tip of her nose, then stepped to the landing with her. Paula was nearly five minutes in her bedroom before coming out: she wore slacks which were not quite large enough for her spreading figure, and had on more lipstick and powder than she needed.

'*So* sorry,' she said hastily. 'I decided at the last minute that pants would be cooler than a skirt today. Aren't you going to wear yours?'

'I haven't time to change.' Janet wore a flowered linen dress with a green background, and sandals but no stockings.

Roger returned to the bedroom when they had gone, hearing Paula talking energetically, and the slamming of the front gate. He felt tired, although nothing like so weary as he had grown used to being. Nevertheless the prospect of a laze and a doze was pleasant.

He did not want to concentrate too much, although there was much to preoccupy him, even apart from Crummy Parker. Marion's presence near the clearing still looked odd, to say the least of it, and Mark's attitude towards Marion somewhat unexpected; it might prove embarrassing.

He went to sleep within five minutes of laying down, and was still asleep when Marion and Mark returned.

When eventually he did wake, he could hear them talking on the lawn at the back of the cottage. There was nothing deep in it, only banter and good-humoured repartee: yet Roger found it disconcerting. Despite his assurances to Paula, Mark rarely lowered his defences quite so completely to any woman.

Marion *was* unusually attractive; Roger admitted that in a detached frame of mind, for he was more than happy with Janet and unconsciously compared everyone else with her, always in her favour. Still, he thought, it was not surprising that Mark was impressed; what mattered was whether Marion was reliable, or whether by some freak of chance she was embroiled in Riordon's affairs.

'Damn it, no!' he muttered with some irritation. 'There isn't the slightest reason for thinking she might be. She could have been wearing rubber shoes anyhow – I'll have to check that. The turf was pretty springy, and we probably wouldn't have heard her walk past if Parker hadn't been there.'

He did not find it wholly satisfying, but had an uncomfortable feeling that he was about to be plunged into an even fiercer maelstrom of events than had preceded his immersion in the Thames, and the fact that he was not wholly fit worried him. There were other disturbing factors. He had no idea what was happening in London, and it was even possible that someone else had been given charge of the case in his absence: it could become more than temporary charge. Possibly Chatsworth would decide that he, West, had had enough of Count Riordon, and that it was time someone else took over. He would have been more reassured had messages from Chatsworth come with greater frequency, but except for the letter about Mark he heard nothing that day.

Nor did anything reach him for the next three days.

By the third day he was seriously contemplating returning to town, although he did not say so to Janet: that would not be wise until within an hour or two of him leaving. The possibility of important events brewing, even of Riordon making further moves against the authorities, grew more than worrying – almost into an obsession.

He hid his feelings from all except Janet, whom he judged likely to be half-expecting him to say that he could stand the false peace of Hinton Magna no longer. Mark had lost himself completely in Marion; at any other time Roger would have been amused and secretly delighted; now the doubts about Marion that would not altogether disperse, tinged his amusement with a touch of wariness, and eschewed any feeling of delight.

Mark's hand was dressed each morning by a little District Nurse, a north-country woman who had lived in Dorset long enough to have overcome suspicions and prejudices. She declared each morning that the improvement was noticeable, and by the end of the third day Mark could move his fingers with much more freedom, although they were still tender. The whole of his fingers and knuckles, as well as part of the back of his hand, had turned a greenish purple with black patches. When he thought about it he wondered just what Riordon had been wearing about his stomach.

Riordon seemed a long way removed from Hinton Magna.

Roger went to bed on the third night, the Wednesday, more inwardly troubled than before. The silence from the Yard was no longer tolerable, and he decided that, if no news arrived next morning, he would go to the Yard.

All of them retired early that night, and as there was a moon, it was not really dark at half-past ten. Janet went to sleep quickly, and he could hear her steady breathing. His right hand was held in her left, and from time to time he could feel her breath stirring his hair.

In the distance he heard the hum of an engine.

Very few cars entered Hinton Magna by night, but there were enough not to make it remarkable. He was surprised, however, when the car slowed down and he heard a squeal of brakes outside the cottage.

He stiffened, and Janet stirred in her sleep.

A car door opened and slammed. After a pause, he heard a murmur of voices. Gently disengaging his hand, he pushed back the clothes and stepped to the carpet-covered floor. Janet stirred again and said something sleepily.

'It's all right,' said Roger soothingly.

He reached the window and looked out. The caution of years made him keep to one side so that he could not be seen.

Moonlight swept the countryside in a pale grey light which created great, shapeless shadows: and it shone upon the top of a saloon car standing by the gate. In front of the bonnet two men were just visible, talking in undertones; Roger could not see them clearly, although a picture of Riordon sprang to his mind.

Then the men moved nearer, coming out of the shadows of the hedge, and he uttered a sharp exclamation of surprise.

'What *is* it, darling?' called Janet, now much wider awake.

Roger half-turned. 'Er – it's all right,' he said. 'I think – oh, damn it! I'm sure Chatsworth's outside.'

'Chatsworth!' exclaimed Janet, sitting up abruptly. 'Roger, what on earth is he doing here?'

'Perhaps he wants a holiday too,' said Roger. 'I'll hop down and have a word with him.'

After a long pause, while he put on his dressing gown and pushed his feet into leather slippers, Janet said explosively: 'If he's going to start this nightly business again I'm going to have something to say about it!'

'Hush,' urged Roger. 'They'll hear you.'

The light of the moon through the landing windows made it easy enough for him to negotiate the twisting stairs, and he was walking along the parquet flooring of the hall when footsteps sounded on the porch. He quickened his step, anxious to open the door before Chatsworth knocked or rang the bell and thus disturbed the rest of the household. He only half-succeeded, for Chatsworth was in the act of knocking when Roger opened the door. Consequently the Assistant Commissioner nearly fell against him, and exclaimed in surprise.

'Good evening, sir,' said Roger drily.

Chatsworth recovered his balance, grunted, peered at Roger, and smoothed the back of his head: he was hatless but held a Homburg in his left hand. 'Oh, it's you, is it?'

'I hoped to prevent you from waking the others up,' said Roger. 'Won't you come in, sir?'

'Why'd you think I came down here?' demanded Chatsworth, and stepped inside.

As he led the way to the lounge and drew the curtains, which had not been drawn because they had left the room before needing a light, Roger felt that Chatsworth was in a difficult mood and was likely to be irascible. As far as Roger was concerned there was nothing to be said against that: Chatsworth was more dangerous when he pretended that everything in the garden was lovely.

'Can't we have a light?' growled Chatsworth, and, when Roger pressed the switch, narrowed his eyes against the glare and muttered: 'Why didn't you warn me?'

Roger ignored him and stepped to a Queen Anne cabinet. He took out a decanter of whisky and a syphon of soda. He poured a stiff peg, added soda, and handed it to his Chief.

'Thanks,' said Chatsworth, more affably. A pause, then: 'Why don't you ask me why I've come?' snapped Chatsworth. 'Every other man on my staff would.'

'I took it for granted you would tell me in good time, sir.'

'You did, did you?' growled Chatsworth, and then to Roger's surprise he yawned widely, several times in quick succession. Now that Roger was able to study his Chief more closely he saw that Chatsworth's eyes were very red-rimmed, that he looked tired out.

The fit of yawning over, Chatsworth said abruptly: 'I'm beginning to understand what you felt like. Sleep seems to be a thing of the past. How are you? Better?'

'Much,' said Roger, firmly.

'Fit enough to start in again?'

'Yes, sir.'

'You can't take anything in this case at half-speed, you know,' said Chatsworth. 'Anyhow, we want you back whether you're fit enough or not. I was managing with Chambers, but he's got hay fever. Hay fever!' snorted the AC. 'What's your opinion of Detective Sergeant Sloan?'

'I couldn't ask for a better man, sir,' said Roger promptly.

'So you've a soft spot for him, have you? You're probably right, and he gives me the impression that he knows nearly as much about this case as you do. I had your message about the *Concerto* on the radio. Nothing helpful I'm afraid. A disc jockey in a nostalgic mood, and certainly not connected with Riordon.'

'We'll get a break soon,' said Roger. 'Have you seen this disc jockey?'

'Upon my living say so, West, do you think I have time to interview such men? Of course I haven't seen him. Would you have?'

'I think I'd ask Sloan to see him, sir.'

'Do what you think best,' said Chatsworth, offhandedly. 'All right, now what else was it you sent along? Oh yes, the man Parker. We haven't found him. I wish I hadn't let him go now, but—'

'I've been rather puzzled by that,' admitted Roger.

'I let him go because I thought he was a harmless old reprobate, and the only reports I had on him were that he hadn't been begging lately or getting drunk and disorderly. That was a pretty detailed story he told Lessing, you know. It answered all the questions.'

'Ye-es,' said Roger.

'Confound you, tell me just what you're thinking!' rasped Chatsworth. 'Think I was wrong to let him go?'

'In the circumstances I should have had him watched, at least. But Riordon was known to live in Queen's Street for some time, and a lot of people would get to know him. There was nothing particularly suspicious about Parker's story, but—' he shrugged his shoulders. 'He certainly wasn't down here by accident, and I don't think he followed Lessing to get the money that was due to him. He would have visited this cottage had he intended to do that, and he would have had some trouble in explaining how he managed to find the address.'

'H'm, yes,' grunted Chatsworth. 'Now what about that map? Do you still think there's a chance that Riordon is looking for it? You sent a note to me about Lessing's idea on that, remember?'

'The more I think about it the more likely it seems,' Roger assured him. 'If my wallet was stolen by an ordinary dip, then the map might be anywhere – probably burned, or thrown away on a refuse heap. The thief wouldn't have kept it after he'd taken the money out.'

Chatsworth stared. 'Is that the best you can do?'

'I don't quite follow you, sir,' said Roger, and, although he gave no hint of it, he felt that Chatsworth was now getting to the crux of his story, the real reason for this late call. He had kept his curiosity in check, but it increased as he saw Chatsworth's narrowed eyes and pursed lips.

'Haven't you any other ideas about the wallet?' demanded the AC sharply.

'We-ell, only vague ones,' admitted Roger. 'I have wondered whether another interested party – say someone who is trying to get at Riordon without our help – had anything to do with it. Or even someone working with Riordon but aiming to take over his authority. That's all very vague, I'm afraid, but—'

'It's right,' said Chatsworth abruptly. 'The private inquiry man we told you about has seen Riordon again. Riordon wanted information about the map. The agent told him it had been stolen from you. Riordon apparently guessed at once who had taken it, left as abruptly as he left Lessing the other night, and—'

Chatsworth paused, as if even he found it difficult to wind up what he had to say, and Roger's tension increased unbearably. 'Well, he didn't get the map back,' finished Chatsworth. 'I've got it. But he's taken one more of our atom scientists. Two others are being threatened, the daughter of another is missing. We can't let this go on much longer, West. We *must* find Riordon's headquarters. We must, do you understand?'

Three Suspects

'I'VE REALISED that for some time, sir,' said Roger.

He spoke after a long pause, in which he had reflected with relief that there was no danger of the case being handed over to anyone else. This visit, especially so late at night, told him a great deal. Amongst it was the obvious fact that Chatsworth had been desperately worried by recent developments and had decided that the only way to find out whether Roger was fit enough to resume work was to come to see him.

The recovery of the pencilled map was another major point. It would surely be possible to find a topographer who would be able to identify the places on it, even though the search might take some time. But the kernel of the visit was what had accompanied the finding of the map.

Chatsworth took his wallet from his pocket and took out the sketch. It was on a slip of paper no larger than an ordinary private correspondence envelope, and the lines and dots on it were in ink. Moreover the sketch, although hastily done, had been drawn by a man who knew how to use pen or pencil.

'I've felt jittery ever since I've had the thing,' he said. 'I should have had it photographed, but I was in a hurry.' If Roger had made such an admission – that a vital piece of evidence had not been properly looked after – Chatsworth would have blown up. 'That's how the case affects all of us, I suppose. Now, I've told you that Riordon created the impression that he knew who had taken it from you. He gave Pep Morgan no idea of the name of the man, but Morgan, who is proving very useful indeed, recovered in time to follow Riordon. You know the way the man ignores – absolutely *ignores* – danger from us? He walks about as if he had an unblemished reputation, confound him.'

'But we know why that is,' said Roger.

'Yes, yes,' said Chatsworth. 'That makes it worse, not better. Where was I? Oh yes, Morgan followed him. He made three calls. Apparently he found nothing after the first two, or he would not have made the third, but that isn't certain. Are you ready for a shock?'

'I think I can stand it, sir.'

'I hope you can,' growled Chatsworth. 'One of the troubles is that everything seems more sinister than it need do in this business, but you probably know that as well as I do. His first call was at the Admiralty. He had a forged pass.'

Roger had a vision of that rabbit warren of offices and passages, and of Riordon going inside.

'Well?'

'He went to the Admiralty,' repeated Chatsworth. 'And he came out without any trouble. I've checked up since, of course. He went to the office of a Commander Morris. Do you know him?'

'The name is vaguely familiar.'

'Anti-atomic submarine research,' said Chatsworth. 'Sound man as far as we know, brilliant in some respects, responsible for much good work. But he went there and Morris saw him. Morris denies it – not very good, is it?'

'It's pretty bad,' admitted Roger.

'Riordon came out, bold as brass, then went across the road to the Home Office buildings. He saw Sir William Bennett. Exactly the same story. Bennett denies it, but our inquiries elicited the fact that he was in his office, alone, when Riordon went there. Similar situation to that of Morris, of course, and most unsatisfactory. Bennett is a good man, a *very* good man. One of the better kind of Civil Servant,' added Chatsworth, 'and not a "do-everything-by-red-tape" slave. We don't know what

Riordon said to either him or Morris, but we do know that Riordon came out and then went a little further afield.' Chatsworth sounded dazed. 'He went to Broadcasting House. It's nearly as difficult to get in there without a permit as it is either of the other places, but Riordon waved his magic wand and went up to Michison's office. Lionel Michison – even *you* know him.'

'Yes,' said Roger. 'He is the producer of many of the variety programmes. I—' he stopped abruptly, but did not say what had entered his mind, for Chatsworth went on: 'Michison says *exactly* the same as the other two – that he did not see Riordon and knows nothing about him. Well, in some circumstances I might be inclined to believe all three, and in others I might be tempted to think that they are victims of Riordon, and therefore too frightened to make any report. However, there's something else I don't like at all. I'll digress a moment. Morgan, by then, had telephoned the Yard. Three Special Branch men went over to the Home Office and followed Riordon to Broadcasting House. There's no doubt about what followed.'

He paused, and Roger watched intently, his mind groping for the significance of these new facts. Chatsworth glanced absently at the whisky before going on: 'One of our men decided to try to tackle Riordon. They followed him into St James' Park and surrounded him. Riordon did what we would expect, and started to fight. In the fight one of our men managed to get everything out of his breast pocket, but before it was over Riordon had floored the others. Among the things in the pocket was that map – it *is* the original, isn't it?'

'Oh yes,' said Roger, who had seen his mark on it. 'There's no doubt at all.'

'Riordon didn't have it when he started out,' said Chatsworth, 'but he did when he was tackled. Consequently we know that it came from Bennett, Morris or Michison. And in turn that means that one or the other of them, probably Michison for it's doubtful whether Riordon would have made the third call for the sake of it, arranged to get it stolen from you. Now do you see why I'm so worried?'

'I do indeed,' said Roger.

It was easy to imagine the reaction to the fact that it was now proved that Riordon had contacts in the Admiralty, the Home Office, and the BBC. Moreover, it was almost impossible to comprehend how far the ramifications of those contacts might go. Again he felt aghast at the calm confidence of Riordon, his utter conviction that no matter what he did or where he went he would not be in danger.

'I'm glad you do,' said Chatsworth. 'What are you thinking of doing? How long before you can start work again?'

'About seven hours,' said Roger. 'What will you do for the night, sir?'

'There's a pub of some kind in the village, isn't there?'

'Yes, but they probably won't appreciate being called up in the early hours.' Roger hesitated. 'I *think* there's a small room here which you could use, if you don't mind cramped quarters? I'm sure Mrs Dean won't mind.'

'Nor do I,' said Chatsworth, and his eyes twinkled. 'D'you mean she won't mind being cramped?'

Dutifully Roger smiled as he went out of the room.

He fancied that he heard a rustle of movement in the passage or on the stairs, but could not be sure. Stepping cautiously past nooks and crannies and places in the shadow, he went upstairs. The rustling came again, this time ahead of him. He thought of Marion Byrne, tried to dismiss the thought, and then heard a door creak.

Could Marion be at the cottage? Or any intruder?

He opened the door of his room, and the creaking of the door when it closed was identical with the sound that he had heard a moment before.

Janet was in bed, breathing heavily and pretending to be asleep. The moonlight was bright enough for him to see that her eyes were moving a little under the lids. He put his head on one side, and said slowly: 'That won't do, sleepwalker.'

'Er?' murmured Janet. 'Eh?' She widened her eyes. 'Why,

darling, I've been asleep again!' Her tone was one of utter innocence.

'Asleep and awake,' said Roger. 'If you'd been a second or two later getting in the room I should probably have jumped on your back. How much did you hear?'

Janet gave up her attempt at deception. 'Not much, darling, and after all, I'm only human. Did you say something about Sir Guy having the little room for the night?'

'I came to ask you if you knew whether the bed's made up.'

He did not show that he was seriously concerned because Janet had overheard much of the conversation. He could hardly blame her; officially he was on the sick list, and even at Fulham her interest in his cases had been keen. Often he had made a habit of talking some aspects of them over with her. In this one the ever-present shadow of Riordon made him particularly anxious not to implicate her in any way: not only would the details make her more disturbed than usual, but it might lead to danger for her.

The spare bed was ready.

When Chatsworth had been down for his case, parked his car, and taken the tiny spare room, Roger and Janet returned to the larger bedroom. Janet took off her dressing gown, eyeing Roger as he stood looking out of the window. 'He's rather a dear,' she remarked.

Roger grunted. 'Is he? He's a bounder in some respects, and if he's listening in I can't help it. I'm going to London tomorrow,' he added shortly.

'You'd better come away from the window then, and get to bed. You don't want to start tired out.'

Roger turned to look at her. 'And no objections from you?'

'You were very decent about me coming downstairs,' said Janet demurely. Then her mood changed. 'Darling, you'll be careful, won't you? Terribly careful?'

'Terribly, terribly careful,' Roger said.

He had never meant anything more.

Odd about that, Roger thought, when he was in bed. Riordon

had beaten off an attack from several men but had surrendered that which he had been most anxious to take away with him. And Riordon did not usually walk about London ignorant of the fact that he was being followed. The harmonica player was not often caught napping. Roger wished that he could follow the workings of the man's mind. It was just possible that Riordon had paid the three visits in order to mislead the police – but there seemed no reasonable grounds for considering that seriously.

When Roger woke, just after seven o'clock, he wondered what had disturbed him so early. His travelling clock, propped up on the table by the side of the bed, told him the time. Then he heard a faint booming noise, and a few minutes afterwards the voice of a BBC announcer.

'Big Ben,' he said half to himself. 'My clock's fast.'

The news, heard vaguely, was not startling, and his thoughts settled on the problem confronting him. On the previous evening he had been quick to see the possible association between Michison of the BBC and the harmonica player who had rendered the *Concerto* so well. If Riordon had influence with Michison it was just possible that he had been able to arrange for that piece to be played. If he had, why had he chosen it at that time?

Roger found himself more than usually perturbed as the vista widened. The tune was a signal, a danger signal; but it need not always represent danger, and it was just possible that Riordon had contrived to send a message via the BBC.

'It's too circumstantial,' muttered Roger, 'and probably has no real foundation, anyhow.'

Nevertheless the possibility troubled him.

Janet woke up soon afterwards, and then Paula's maid brought in some morning tea. While drinking, and taking the bull by the horns, Roger broached the subject of Janet staying at the cottage for a week.

'It's not that I won't miss you, but—'

'You'll be able to concentrate on taking risks, darling. All right, I—'

A scream cut across her words.

It was a high-pitched feminine scream, and whoever it was seemed terrified. Roger flung back the clothes and jumped out of bed: the corner of his pyjama jacket caught a cup and sent it flying. He opened the door, with the crash of breaking crockery on the floor echoing in his ears, to see the maid pointing towards the little room. The door of it was open, and Paula was coming out of her bedroom, dustcap in hand.

'There's a man!' screamed the maid. 'A man – in there!'

'A man – oh, a *man*,' echoed Roger, suddenly comprehending.

He soothed the girl while explaining to Paula what liberties he had taken with her spare room, and while he was in the middle of it Chatsworth appeared, clad in a mackintosh. He was a vast and burly figure with his little fringe of hair sticking out at the sides, looking much thicker than it normally appeared. He apologised graciously to the maid for scaring her, as charmingly thanked Paula for her unwitting but, he was sure, quite willing hospitality. Paula fell for him at once.

Mark was the last to get up.

Roger was not surprised to find him sore at being allowed to sleep during the talk with Chatsworth: nor was he surprised when Mark, with unusual lack of insistence, agreed that in view of the trouble with his hand he could not do a great deal in London.

'I should say your hand will keep you out of it for another three days, including today,' said Roger. 'Marion *is* leaving on Friday, isn't she?'

Mark had the grace to colour.

With characteristic cunning, Chatsworth called a meeting of four soon after breakfast, and the lounge was put at their disposal. As well as himself, Roger and Mark, Sloan was at the conference, and Chatsworth gave a brief résumé of what he had told Roger the previous evening, to smooth any ruffled feelings on Mark's part. The discussion veered round to the map before long, and Chatsworth sought in his pocket for his wallet, took it out, and said reflectively: 'It's *just* possible that the venue is somewhere near here, I suppose. Anyhow, one of you might have more luck than West did in identifying the place. Where *is* the damn thing?' He took a dozen or more papers from his wallet, dropping them to an occasional table and frowning. 'I *know* I put it in here,' he went on, and then looked sharply at Roger. 'Or did I give it to you?'

'You put it back in there,' Roger assured him.

'I thought I did,' said Chatsworth. He took every paper from the wallet, unfolding some to see whether the map had slipped in between the folds. As he searched the tension grew greater, and before he finished Mark said sharply: 'Can it have been stolen?'

No one answered until Chatsworth finished the search, put the empty wallet down by the little pile of papers, and said very slowly: 'It's not here.'

'Then it has been stolen,' Mark said softly.

'But who took it?' asked Roger, very slowly. 'Sloan, you've watched the house all night, haven't you? No one's been here?'

'I've seen no one,' said Sloan after a pause. 'Except—'

'It can't have been anyone in the house!' said Mark.

The tension reached its peak: each man looked at the next, uncertain and anxious. Chatsworth began to go through his other pockets but found no map, and when he had finished he looked keenly at the fresh-faced, ingenuous-looking Sloan, and said with deceptive softness: 'Didn't you make an exception, Sloan?'

'Yes, sir,' said the sergeant stiffly and formally. He did not look towards Mark, while in Roger's mind a question was already forming, one which worried him the more because he could see no reasonable explanation of it.

'For whom?'

'Miss Marion Byrne called a little before seven o'clock,' answered Sloan in the same level voice. 'She told me that she had left her handbag here last night and was a little worried because it had most of her money in it, as well as some personal papers.'

Mark stared at the man without speaking.

'Did she find it?' Chatsworth demanded.

'She said so, sir. She went round to the rear of the house and when she came back she said she had found it in the loggia. She said she remembered leaving it somewhere in the garden, that was why she was so worried. I'm telling you what she said as nearly as I can, sir.'

'Yes, yes,' said Chatsworth. 'Where's the window of my room, West?'

'Immediately above the loggia,' Roger answered.

A brief inspection of the back of the cottage showed that it would be easy for anyone to climb to the roof of the loggia and step into the little spare bedroom. Moreover there was a small chair, over which Chatsworth had hung his coat, within easy reach of the window.

Chatsworth watched the inspection without speaking, and if he noticed that Mark looked very pale, said nothing. But when they had finished, and the obvious possibilities were faced, Chatsworth spoke very softly: 'In future, West, I'll leave *this* kind of business to you. If any man in the Force had been so damned careless I would have stopped his promotion for three years. But here—'

'I might have put it under my pillow, but nothing more than that,' said Roger shortly. 'Of course, we're taking too much for granted about Miss Byrne. Someone else might have got to your window, slipping through without being noticed. Only two men were watching, and the night was quite dark once the moon went down. All the same we'd better go to the Manor.' He avoided Mark's eyes.

'Take Sloan with you,' directed Chatsworth.

Mark made no effort to follow them, but sat back in his chair as they left the room.

The warmth of the morning was already enough to make them perspire, and they went quickly. Roger was thinking of the coincidence of Marion's first appearance on the scene when he turned into the drive of the Manor. There he stopped, for cycling along the road from the village was the local policeman. The man was in uniform, red-faced, perspiring freely. He drew up with them and said breathlessly: 'You – you're Inspector West, sir, aren't you? From Scotland Yard?'

'That's right,' said Roger. 'What's the trouble?'

'I don't rightly know, sir,' said the constable. 'Mr Byrne just telephoned me. He—he said something about murder, sir.'

'Whose murder?' snapped Roger, his heart missing a beat.

'I—I don't rightly know, sir. I'm just going to make my inquiries now, before I telephone to Dorchester.'

'Let's get on,' said Roger sharply.

The constable pushed his bicycle, the others strode by his side. Roger had a vision of Marion Byrne as the victim of the murder, although he tried to push it aside. Once they rounded a bend in the drive they saw signs of activity, including three or four people standing near the porch of the big Georgian House and others by one of the windows. Roger did not see Marion, but recognised Colonel Byrne, her uncle. Byrne was a tall, thin, sallow man, a martinet and a stickler for convention.

Before anyone spoke Roger saw a heap on the ground; the heap took shape, and as he drew nearer he saw that what at first looked like a heap of old clothes was in fact the body of a man; at a distance of fifty yards he recognised Crummy Parker.

Roger West Returns to Town

THERE WAS NO doubt that Parker was dead, or that he had been murdered. The side of his head was battered in, and while Roger admitted the bare possibility that it was the result of a fall from the window above, his opinion was that the wounds had been caused by a weapon – the universal blunt instrument. He told Sloan to try to find Marion, and suggested to the Hinton Magna constable that the quicker he telephoned his headquarters the better; and he asked whether a doctor had been summoned.

In a thin, reedy voice, Colonel Byrne said that he had taken all the usual measures, and demanded by what authority Inspector West had to make inquiries without first consulting the county police.

'Common sense,' said Roger shortly. Then he realised that he was being too abrupt. 'Actually, sir, this man is wanted by us in London.'

'Then perhaps you can be good enough to tell me what he is doing here?' Byrne said tartly.

Roger eyed Marion's uncle with distaste: at close quarters Byrne's face looked raddled, his eyes were bloodshot, and the hue of his bony nose suggested that he was a heavy drinker. But there was no hint of anxiety or concern in the man's manner, and Roger prevented himself from drawing Byrne into the orbit of his suspicions. He remained sceptical of Marion Byrne's part in the affair, too. It was carrying coincidence too far to believe that he and the others had come to recuperate on the very doorstep of intrigue.

Byrne strode off, declaring that he would talk to the Chief Constable, while Roger inquired how the tramp had been found and whether anyone had any idea how long he had been dead. He knew that it had been a comparatively short time, and was not surprised when an old man, wrinkled of face and quavery of speech, came forward and admitted: 'I saw un an hour since, sir.'

'Was he just here?' asked Roger.

'Wouldn't like to say so,' said the old man slowly. 'Round an' about, mebbe. Walking. I shouted at un to go away, an' off he went like a dog with his tail 'tween his legs, sir. I come round this way again, and there he was lying, stiff as they make 'em. 'Tis all I can tell 'ee, sir.'

'Thank you,' said Roger. 'It's a great help.'

He had further assistance from others of the staff at the Manor, who were eager to talk and did not appear to share the Colonel's prejudice against his prompt inquiries. A maid who had come from the village, being a day worker only, had imagined that she had seen Parker at a window, climbing in or out, she would not be sure which. A maid in the house had heard a thump, three quarters of an hour earlier, and going out immediately, had seen Parker in a huddled heap on the ground. Except to turn him over to try to find whether there was any spark of life the man had not been touched. There were bruises on his legs, Roger saw, consistent with a fall from the window, but his opinion was that Parker had been struck over the head, made to release his grip on the window, fallen, and died almost as soon as he had struck the ground.

Deliberately he avoided mentioning Marion Byrne, although he half-expected to hear her name mentioned when he asked which room the tramp had fallen from: he was disappointed in one way and relieved in another. The window from which the man had fallen was from a landing: there was no evidence to say whom Parker had been trying to see.

'But he was almost certainly attacked while inside the house,' mused Roger.

Sloan was a long time putting in an appearance, and before he returned from his inquiries, which Roger knew would be made with the utmost deliberation, a doctor arrived from Hinton Parva, the neighbouring village. The doctor was a Scotsman, short, crisp of hair, and sharp of speech. He looked tired and harassed, Roger thought, and in the course of the next half-hour discovered that the medico had been out three times during the night.

No one seemed to be able to get enough sleep, Roger reflected, and was duly sympathetic.

Dr Hamilton would not commit himself, but voiced the same opinion: Parker had been struck over the head when at the window, had lost his hold, fallen and bruised himself, and died without recovering consciousness; death had probably come very quickly after he had been struck. Roger had no quarrel with that report, and began to speculate upon Byrne's reaction when he knew that the house would have to be searched for a weapon and that there was at least a reasonable excuse for suspecting one or other of the occupants.

Marion's continued absence puzzled Roger, but he deliberately evaded mentioning her.

A dapper Inspector from Dorchester arrived within an hour of being telephoned, and any fear that Roger had of having trouble with the County CID quickly faded. Inspector Cartwright declared himself delighted that Inspector West was so fortuitously near, and asked for guidance. In a very short time Cartwright had seen Byrne, politely but effectively silenced his protests, and arranged for a complete search of the house. Convinced that the local investigations were in good hands, Roger waited only to tell Cartwright that there was reason to believe that the case was an offshoot of one even more serious, and then went in search of Sloan. After ten minutes he discovered the sergeant drinking tea in the large, gloomy kitchen of the Manor. Sloan was laughing and talking with the cook, but detached himself from her soon after Roger put his head round the door. They met outside the domestic entrance to the house.

'Well?' asked Roger shortly.

'Miss Byrne hasn't been seen this morning, sir,' said Sloan.

'Not at all?'

'I don't think I've missed anyone,' said Sloan. 'She's very popular with all the staff, and there is a spot of bother going on at the moment. Apparently the Colonel told Miss Byrne that she was spending too much time at the cottage, and there was a difference of opinion.' He went on slowly: 'The general impression is that she left here deliberately, and the staff seem to think that she will move to the cottage.'

'I don't like it, Bill,' Roger said slowly.

'Nor will Mr Lessing, sir.'

'No. Have you had the slightest reason for thinking that Miss Byrne might be involved in any way – apart from the scare I raised because she was near Mr Lessing and me on Monday?'

'None at all, sir.' Sloan brushed his crisp, fair hair back from his forehead, and regarded Roger with a puzzled frown. 'It's got me beat.'

'We needn't be formal, Sir Guy isn't round the corner.'

Roger saw the appreciative smile in Sloan's eyes, and remembered Chatsworth's question about the sergeant: Sloan was almost certainly earmarked for promotion, and would soon rank as Detective Inspector. Roger was glad, for he had worked with Sloan for years and knew that the man was sound, sometimes brilliant, and always painstaking.

'You can't always be sure where he'll be next,' Sloan said.

'We'll take a chance now,' said Roger. He proffered cigarettes and added as Sloan struck a match: 'Have you anything up your sleeve about Miss Byrne?'

'No,' said Sloan. 'I've tried assuming that she is mixed up in it somewhere, but I always come to the same dead-end. If she were just a friend of the family it would be different, although even then we'd have to stretch a point. But she's at the Manor every year, and I can't make myself believe that you just chanced upon a place where Riordon has an agent. I've inquired about when she first arranged to come here this week, too. The servants knew about it last Monday, so presumably the Colonel and his wife knew earlier than that.'

'Good,' said Roger briskly. 'We count her out, then, except that she might have been approached by one of Riordon's people, and persuaded to help them. We mustn't rule out that possibility, even though it's hardly probable. Next?'

Sloan shrugged. 'I'd be inclined to say that Parker stole the map, passed it over to a confederate, and then tried to get into the house. That could have been on an ordinary burglary, of course, but—'

Roger shook his head.

'I think it's doubtful, too,' admitted Sloan. 'Well, then, how's this? Parker stole the map, and delivered it to someone in the house. The rendezvous was the landing window. Parker handed the map over, and was killed to prevent him from talking.'

'Better,' conceded Roger, 'but I can see the improbabilities. I can't imagine anyone who has any right to be in the Manor making an appointment to see Parker at a first floor window, especially in daylight and at an hour when many of the servants would be about. It's more likely that Parker was admitted by one of the doors, or else entered through a ground floor window and then realised that he had to get away in a hurry. Before he managed it he was assaulted. It's easy to imagine him reaching the window in something of a panic. Riordon can create a panic in a brave man, you know.'

Sloan said sharply: 'Riordon himself?'

'I don't see why not,' said Roger. 'But it might have been anyone who could have done Parker some harm. Parker saw that the stairs were barred by Riordon or whoever it was, and came to the window. He wouldn't climb out face first, very few people climb out of a window that way: he would climb out backwards. While swaying on the window sill he could do nothing to save himself from being hit.' Roger paused, tapped the ash from his cigarette, and went on: 'Well, how does it sound?'

'Very reasonable,' admitted Sloan. 'But we're up against the old problem, aren't we? Who hit him? Had whoever hit him any right to be there? If so we strike that coincidence again, and I can't say I'm keen on it.'

'I don't necessarily grant you that there is one. If it were Riordon himself he wouldn't have hesitated to break into any house where he wanted to get.'

'But why *here*?' demanded Sloan.

Roger was quiet for a moment.

There was no one in sight, although the sound of men moving about the other side of the house was intermittent, and twice cars came along the drive. A clock in the house chimed the half-hour. A wasp honed about Sloan's head, and the sergeant brushed at it two or three times.

'Riordon almost certainly discovered that we were here,' Roger said slowly. 'Even if he didn't follow me he could have followed Lessing – or even Sir Guy. Let's assume that it was Lessing. He would learn quickly about Marion Byrne, probably from Parker, who I think worked with him. That's by no means certain yet.'

'Supposing Riordon did know about Miss Byrne?' Sloan was puzzled.

Roger threw a half-finished cigarette away, grinding it into the earth, and said sharply: 'You aren't at your best, Bill, are you? Riordon's always specialised in victimising pretty women, presumably when they have been in a position to help him, directly or otherwise. Lessing and Marion have been seen about so much together that most people would judge that they'd been smitten. Marion could be in a position to give information through Lessing.'

Sloan drew in a deep breath. 'Of course! I hope Lessing doesn't think of that too soon.'

'So do I,' said Roger fervently. 'So do I.' But he did not think that it would take Mark long to reach the same conclusion, and he was in a gloomy mood as he left the Manor, a little after eleven o'clock. He was quite sure that he could safely leave the investigation at the house in the hands of Cartwright, although two Yard men, then on duty near the cottage, would be at hand to assist the Dorchester police. He had learned that neither Byrne nor his wife were surprised to find that Marion had gone, and he judged that Mrs Byrne was worried in a fluttering, half-hearted way; she was but a vague background to her husband. He disliked the Colonel, but could not bring himself to believe that he was in any way implicated: the simpler and more straightforward explanation seemed more likely.

After lunch and an interview with Chatsworth, he decided that Riordon or an accomplice had been to Hinton Magna, made contact with Parker, heard about Marion, and visited her in the early hours. After that Marion had left the Manor and gone to the cottage, but whether to take the map could not be unanswered.

'Riordon could have frightened her into doing that,' said Roger quietly.

Chatsworth said: 'The less we credit Riordon with, the better we'll fight him, West.'

'If we underestimate him, we'll be in trouble,' Roger countered. He paused, and when Chatsworth did not retort, went on: 'What attitude would you like me to adopt with Lessing, sir?'

'Please yourself,' said Chatsworth shortly. 'He's no fool, and he knows enough now to make it useless to try to hoodwink him.'

Roger went up to Mark's room.

The whole atmosphere of the cottage had changed since the morning. The happiness which had ruled was gone, and it was remarkable that Paula talked in exaggerated whispers, rarely raising her voice. Janet was subdued, and Mark stayed in his room most of the time. Roger was puzzled by the way his friend reacted, but relieved when he saw a crooked smile on Mark's face as he entered the room.

'Well, Mister Policeman,' Mark said. 'Take a pew. Now,

what's the official verdict?'

'Postponed,' said Roger.

'I suppose that's inevitable.' Mark took out his cigarette case and tapped a cigarette on his thumbnail. 'Y'know, Roger, if you try from now until Christmas you'll never convince me that Marion took that map.'

'I don't propose to try, yet.'

'I thought that was where you'd start from,' said Mark. 'It *is* the obvious starting point, old man. I've been trying to think of another, although I'm damned if I can. Anyhow, if you've an open mind I'm glad. What are you going to do now?'

'I'm going back to town with Chatsworth and Sloan,' said Roger. 'Janet's staying here, and I'd like you to keep an eye on her.' He paused. 'Will you?'

'I shall also look for Marion,' said Mark.

'I'd taken that for granted,' said Roger. He punched Mark's shoulder, and added: 'Now if I don't get off the Old Man will start creating, and he's in a touchy mood as it is. If you get any line at all, don't investigate on your own account, but phone me right away. All right?'

'Fair's fair,' said Mark, and shrugged. 'Look after yourself.'

A gloomy parting, thought Roger, and yet not a surprising one. Clearly Mark was very worried indeed lest Riordon had exerted his sinister influence over the girl.

So, thought Roger, am I.

It was nearly eight o'clock that evening when Roger walked up the stairs to his office at the Yard. He shared it with four other Chief Inspectors, and wondered whether any of them would be there. They would have hurried away at the slightest chance of an evening off, although leisure had become a rarity for the police; there was not enough staff to cope with London's crime.

Sitting at a light oak desk near the window was a portly, heavily-built man with a preoccupied expression on a perky face. He wore a light grey suit which fitted badly, and sported a red-spotted tie. His chin receded a little and his forehead slanted, so that his rather pointed and large nose looked like the apex of a wide-based triangle. Casual acquaintances frequently rated Chief Inspector Eddie Day as a man of no consequence, and few found it easy to believe that he was a Chief Inspector at the Yard. Yet his opinions on forged treasury notes and false coins was not only respected; it was revered. Eddie spent his life unravelling the mysteries of forgeries, and the complications and difficulties which ensued gave him a worried, almost harassed manner. His pet aversion was the calligraphic 'expert'. He had no regard for their judgement on handwriting unless they were prepared to corroborate his testimony, and had little enthusiasm then.

He did not look round when the door opened, but continued to stare into the large, bare courtyard, with an elbow on the desk and his hand supporting his chin.

'Fast asleep?' asked Roger.

'Eh?' Day turned abruptly, his elbow slipping. 'Why, Handsome, I didn't expect to see you! How are you, old son, how are you?' Eddie pushed his chair back, rose, and proffered a warm hand. 'Not much the worse for wear, eh?' Gravely he examined the patch of plaster, and shook his head. 'You do get into trouble don't you? One of these days you'll get your pretty face spoiled, and what will your wife say then?' He beamed widely, showing prominent but very white teeth. 'Seriously, old boy, how are you?'

'About as I look,' said Roger. 'How's business?'

'Not very good,' said Eddie, shaking his hand and transforming his smile into a frown. 'Not very good at all, Handsome. It's a bad time for slush, all people seem to forge these days are football pool coupons and raffle tickets. And there's no *depth* about that kind of thing. No *body,* if you see what I mean.' He sat down, as Roger went to his own desk and frowned at a pile of buff-coloured papers upon it. A great deal had accumulated, mostly work which had nothing to do with the Riordon affair and which he would have preferred to leave alone. 'I know what you mean,' he said absently.

'I ought to tell you that Chambers has been messing about at your desk,' said Eddie. 'The AC put him in charge and he went through your stuff for anything about the Riordon business. Didn't get much, as far as I could see. I say, old man' – Eddie looked at once eager and reluctant – 'the AC's been raising hell ever since you went. You haven't seen him yet, have you? Three times I heard him say that he wanted you to go straight to his office when you came back. You haven't been putting your foot in it, have you?'

Roger looked up with a grin. 'That squib's damp, Eddie.'

'You mean you've seen him?'

'And I remain alive and unmolested,' said Roger. 'Eddie, I'd hate to be rude, but I've a lot to do.'

'Oh, all right, all right,' said Eddie aggrievedly. 'I only thought I'd warn you. Well, I may as well go home. Cheer-i-bye.'

He collected a bowler hat and an umbrella, and went out, Roger saying 'Good night' absently.

For the next half-hour he ran through reports on various minor cases, most of which had been dealt with in his absence. There was little of importance, although the account of the Court proceedings after a raid on a nightclub made him scowl: the owner and the staff had deserved twelve months inside, but had escaped with a fine. Either the magistrate had felt extremely lenient or the case had been badly presented. He discovered that the victim of hay fever, Chambers, had guided it through the Court and shrugged his shoulders. Five people were out of jail because a man had a severe bout of hay fever.

The routine jobs finished, Roger picked up a manilla folder marked 'Riordon', and then made himself familiar with various reports which had come in, but of which Chatsworth had mentioned only a few. There was little outstanding, except the name and address of the woman whose body had been found in the river near the Albert Bridge, and whom he had been going to see when he had been attacked.

There was also a photograph of her.

Roger studied that first. A good-looking woman, he judged, not in her first youth; the photograph betrayed the obvious care with which she had made herself up, and defeated its own object of trying to present an ageless likeness. Thin eyebrows, obviously plucked, a rather short nose, and well-shaped lips with the underlip a little fuller than the upper. Good-looking nevertheless, and her eyes seemed to laugh at him.

The caption typed on a slip of paper and pasted to the back of the photograph read:

Mrs Leo. Clayton. Wife Lt. Commander Clayton R.N. (Submarines)

'Just another of them,' he thought glumly. 'Not much difference from the rest.'

From the report he learned that Clayton was at sea, and had been out of England for nearly eighteen months, serving on a Far East station. He was thirty-nine, his wife two years younger. They were wealthy, and on either side related to well-known families. Ideal victims for Riordon, for they would be anxious to avoid scandal at all cost.

Roger's lips set tightly.

Another man highly placed in secret circles would receive a shock that might break him up. Roger wondered how long it had been since Clayton had heard from his wife, then found a note that she had been missing for six weeks.

Roger finished reading the file, then looked through the report of the three CID men who had gone to Morgan's assistance. Chatsworth had told the story of Michison, Morris and Bennett fully, and there was little to add. Riordon had gone to see each of them, and the evidence that he had actually entered their offices seemed quite conclusive. The verbatim reports of conversations with the men themselves, and their denials that Riordon had been in to see them, were interesting because in each case the man had been very emphatic.

'I'll see 'em myself,' Roger decided, and picked up the

telephone, asking for Sloan. When the sergeant answered, Roger said: 'Sloan, do you know the addresses, private and business, of Michison, Morris and Bennett?'

'There's a note of them in my file,' said Sloan.

'Get in touch with them, and make appointments for me tonight, will you?' asked Roger. 'And have you the name of the harmonica player who performed on the radio the other day?'

'Yes, sir. Reginald Bright. He's in the RAF. I've his number and station here somewhere.'

'Find out the most convenient time for me to see him, will you?' asked Roger.

The air of the *Warsaw Concerto* kept running through his mind. He recalled vividly the effect it had had upon him when he had heard it on the radio after waking up out of a deep sleep in the orchard of the cottage. He could not rid himself of the conviction that the artiste who had played it over the air was the same as Riordon's faithful watchdog.

'But if he's in the RAF he can't be,' said Roger, 'and that's that.'

Chatsworth telephoned to say that there was nothing waiting for him that needed discussing that night, and that he was going to his flat. He wanted Roger to come to see him first thing in the morning. Roger gave the necessary assurance, and then Sloan rang through. 'I've made the appointments, sir,' he said. 'Michison at nine-fifteen, Morris at ten o'clock, and Bennett at ten forty-five.'

'Did you have any trouble?' asked Roger.

'None of them seemed surprised,' said Sloan.

'We'll have to get going if we're to fit them all in.'

'You want me to come with you?'

'Yes. You'll be home late, too.'

Five minutes later he climbed into a ten horsepower car, at the wheel of which Sloan was already sitting, and was told that Michison would be at his flat, only a few blocks away from Broadcasting House. The others would also be at their private residence, both flats within a reasonable distance of Oxford

Street and Portland Place.

'Convenient,' mused Roger. 'We have some luck.'

The approach to the flat of Lionel Michison was anything but impressive. The outside of the house, in a narrow by-street, was grey and dirty, and the door needed painting badly. So did most of London, reflected Roger idly. He relaxed, knowing that he might need to work himself up to a considerable pitch of energy and mental alertness before the night was out, and preferring to take it easy when he could.

Narrow stairs, shadowy in spite of the daylight, landing windows half-blacked out, drab coconut matting on the stairs, all gave an unpleasant, dreary impression of the house. He had not expected to find Michison in such surroundings. That was probably foolish; he knew that BBC officials were not what they sometimes appeared to be to the general public – denizens of a strange, glittering world. But Lionel Michison's voice, familiar to millions, had with it a hint of well-being, carried a faint aura of comfort and culture; Roger had always imagined him to live in a residence as modern as the BBC itseThe flat was at the top of the house, and only one door led from the small, square landing. There was enough light for them to see the bell, and Sloan pressed it. In the shadows, Sloan looked a comfortable, reassuring fellow, a useful man for any emergency.

After a short pause the door opened. Roger was surprised to see a maid in cap and apron, and to catch a glimpse of a small lounge hall furnished on modern lines and striking exactly the impression he had conceived of Michison.

'Is Mr Michison in?' he asked.

'Yes, sir. Are you Inspector West?'

'That's right,' said Roger.

'He would like you to wait just a few minutes, sir,' said the woman. She was middle-aged, neatly dressed, prim in appearance and in voice. 'He won't keep you long.'

'That's all right,' said Roger. The maid walked from the lounge, after asking them to sit down, and disappeared. A door, painted black with red lines running about it, closed without a sound; several others led from the hall. The carpet was red, its pile luxurious. There were some black-and-white cartoons on the wall, originals by well-known artists and all caricatures of star performers over the air.

They waited for perhaps five minutes before a door opened.

Prior to that they heard the soft strains of music, probably from a radio, coming from one of the rooms. With the opening of the door the strains grew louder. No one appeared, and the door might have been opened by some hidden mechanism. Roger stared towards it, and Sloan followed his gaze. The piece, coming so softly and gently, was Brahms' *Lullaby,* yet it had the effect of putting them at a tension, and was enough to make Roger clench his hands.

Slowly the music faded. No one appeared in the open doorway, but then a fresh tune began, distant at first but fast growing louder and unmistakable. It was the reedy note of a harmonica; and it was the *Warsaw Concerto.*

'I don't like this,' muttered Sloan.

'I hardly expected you to,' said the voice from behind the open door.

They recognised the voice above the swelling volume of the music: it was Riordon's. Roger backed swiftly towards the landing door; it was a spontaneous movement, as was that of his hand towards his right side pocket. He did not feel inside, for Riordon stepped into sight; tall, menacing, staring at them with a ferocious smile as if knowing that he could destroy them, and looking forward to the task.

'The door is locked on the outside,' he said. 'I have arranged it. *Very* good of you to come to see me, West. I knew I would have the pleasure of meeting you again soon. And Sloan as well! I am having a most successful evening.'

He stopped, and stood staring at them.

Surprises from Riordon

THERE WAS NO doubt about it, thought Roger, this man had the ability to frighten. He had only to be himself and he succeeded in creating fear, thus gaining an immediate advantage over anyone who saw him. It was absurd and there was no real cause for it: to let the man gain ascendancy was to play into his hands.

Roger fought against the insidious influence, and did not look away from the pale grey eyes. Sloan seemed to have disappeared; certainly Roger was not aware of his presence; the issue was between himself and Riordon.

'Be matter-of-fact,' he said urgently to himself. 'Matter-of-fact, that's all.'

'Come in,' said Riordon. 'Both of you.'

With an effort, Roger said: 'That's why we came.'

'Oh no,' said Riordon. 'You came to see Michison, as I knew you would. Poor Michison has served his purpose, you needn't worry at all about him. The deluded British public will not have to listen to his affected voice again. I'm sure that soothes you.'

Roger said: 'I rather liked his voice.'

'What a pretty little tea table tittle-tattler you make,' sneered Riordon. 'But it's no use, West. I know you're shaking in your shoes, and so would I if I were in your position.' He laughed. 'I said come in! Don't try to turn and run. You'd never get away.'

Roger said: 'Try the front door, Sloan.'

There was no response and no movement, but the grin on Riordon's face grew more menacing. Roger found it hard to force himself to look away from the man, but he did so to see why Sloan had not obeyed: the possibility that the sergeant was fascinated by Riordon, affected like a rabbit under the eye of a stoat, was the first thing to enter his mind.

'*Come in,*' repeated Riordon thinly.

With a palpable effort Roger looked away, towards the spot where Sloan had been standing. There was no sign of the sergeant: the man had completely disappeared.

He felt cold as he realised that, tried to reassure himself, knowing that somehow Sloan had been taken out of the lounge hall and that the soft pile of the carpet had muffled the sound. But it was uncanny that there had been no intimation of the other's movement. He licked his lips, but did not look at Riordon immediately; he stepped to the landing door and tried the handle. There was no key in the lock, but when he turned the handle the door would not open.

'I don't lie,' said Riordon softly.

Roger swung round and almost knocked into the man, who was standing close by his side. Again that uncanny silence of movement had been demonstrated, enough to frighten him by itself. Damn it, he was *not* frightened, this was just a man, a human being.

Riordon felt his pockets; Roger did nothing to stop him. It was a quick frisk, and Riordon gave the impression that he was used to the process. His smile widened when he stood back and said: 'So you don't carry a gun, West.'

Roger said slowly: 'Only on dangerous jobs.'

'What do you mean?' flashed Riordon sharply.

There was the man's weakness: everyone who had come in contact with him said how vain he was. Riordon's overwhelming vanity, his touchiness when anything was said or done to suggest that he was not supreme in everything he touched. To anger him might prove dangerous, but to placate him would be madness.

Roger smiled. To his relief he found the smile came without too much effort; now that the first shock of the encounter was over he felt much more himself. He thrust a hand in his pocket and said: 'I have to get special permission to carry firearms, and it's only granted when the suspect is likely to be too dangerous to handle without them. I don't rate you so high.'

He walked towards the door, Riordon moving by his side, and heard the man's sharp intake of breath. As he entered the room beyond he heard the last bars of the Concerto, and then a faint rasping noise which first startled and then amused him: there was a radiogram in one corner of the room; the lid was raised and a record was spinning round and round upon the base.

'But your effects aren't bad,' he admitted.

'I have always thought you a fool,' said Riordon slowly. 'I am now quite sure of it. Dangerous! Haven't you the sense to understand what I can *do,* West?'

Roger shrugged. 'Drug a few helpless women and frighten a few doting parents, yes. And other odds and ends.'

He pretended not to be perturbed or impressed by Riordon, and again was relieved that the pretence was fairly easily maintained; he was no longer so scared of the man. Perhaps an additional reason for that was the fact that the room into which he stepped was empty of people. It was a larger lounge, furnished in modern style, making as great a contrast with the staircase and landing outside as the lounge hall had done. Two tall standard lamps with vellum shades stood on either side of a small piano, one of the lights on, the other off. The easy chairs looked comfortable, a small cabinet of inlaid walnut, with books standing on either side of it, was opposite the radiogram; there were delicate water colours on the walls.

On the small mantelpiece, beneath which was an electric fire, were two photographs. One was of a man, the other of a fluffy-haired woman who was smiling and whose charm seemed to spring out of the likeness.

Roger was less interested in her than in the man: it was Lionel Michison, smiling like the woman who was presumably his wife. He had clear-cut features and a thin line of moustache;

there was a friendliness about his expression which Roger liked.

At least it was Michison's flat: there was no trickery in that.

Riordon said slowly: 'You are not making things any easier for yourself, West.'

'Oh, don't be a fool,' said Roger irritably. 'We had to meet like this sooner or later, and I don't mind whether you fixed the appointment or I did. Get it out of your mind that you are the world's mastermind, Riordon.' Watching the man's face he felt that Riordon would soon be worked up into a frenzy, but there was an idea germinating in his mind, and he saw hope if he could develop it properly: the first essential to such development was casualness and self-confidence. If he could only get himself into a frame of mind where he was not alarmed at the immediate prospects, he would be able to carry it off.

'Go on,' said Riordon.

'About what?' asked Roger. He sat down and crossed his legs. 'Why don't you switch that thing off?'

As if taken by surprise, Riordon half-turned, then swung round again. His eyes were blazing, and clearly he had expected Roger to leap at him. Roger took out a case and selected a cigarette carefully, replaced the case and then sought for a match. Riordon backed to the radiogram, and took the record off.

'Thanks,' said Roger. 'Now, this long overdue talk. You seem to have the impression that we're frightened of you, and that we daren't stop you.'

'You certainly daren't,' snapped Riordon.

'No?' Roger raised his eyebrows. 'If I wanted to I could take you with me to the Yard now, but it would spoil our game, and a very pretty and complicated one it is. With you as a pawn, Riordon. You've been a godsend.'

'Are you *mad?*'

'I've thought that about you,' said Roger with a bright smile. 'But as it's been to my advantage why should I worry? Still, you can go too far, and we may have to take you in whether it suits our purpose or not.'

'*Your purpose?*' said Riordon in a strangled voice.

'That's right.'

'I'm not fooled, West, don't think that I am. I know how you are feeling. I know that you and Chatsworth and others at the Yard are frightened to do anything in case the whole story is published. A fine story it will be! Men in high Government positions, highly placed officers in the services, *all* completely under my influence.'

Roger said with great deliberation: 'How foolish can you get?'

He had succeeded in puzzling the man at the cost of infuriating him, and he had sown the seed of uncertainty, which was what he had set out to do. Riordon was on shifting ground, the first breach in the façade of his incredible self-confidence was in the making. It was a reassuring fact, blinding Roger to what might happen before this strange interview ended. He thought uneasily of Sloan again, then he assured himself that the sergeant must be in one of the other rooms of the flat; and set his anxiety aside.

'You really think that?' asked Riordon thinly.

'Aren't we wasting time?' asked Roger testily. 'I don't believe that you seriously think you're the mighty panjandrum. By the way, where is Michison?'

'Where he will do no more harm,' said Riordon sharply. 'And I have had enough of this fool's talk, West. You came to find out why Michison submitted so easily to me, and you are going to see Morris and Bennett, on the same errand. You will be wasting your time. They will not see you.'

'Won't they?'

'They will refuse to see you,' repeated Riordon. 'Immediately I heard what you were going to do I gave them orders not to allow the interviews.'

'Oh.' Roger looked slightly put out. 'And how did you come to know about it?'

'They told me,' said Riordon sharply. 'They telephoned me

immediately after you called them about the visit, and I gave them very careful instructions. I had less faith in Michison than either of the others, and made different arrangements for him. Would you like to see those arrangements, West?'

'Not particularly,' said Roger. 'Riordon, I—' He stopped abruptly.

While remaining wary, he had felt much more sure of himself for some minutes past, although he was watching every movement that the other made. Yet Riordon made none then, and did not even look beyond Roger's shoulder. Yet there was a movement behind him, although he had felt quite sure that no one else was in the room.

He schooled himself not to look round, but could not prevent the break in his voice. The movement persisted, but Riordon continued to look at him. Through the temporary silence there came a faint whispering sound, and then, unmistakably, the strains of the *Concerto*.

Riordon started.

'Isn't that the signal for you to skedaddle?' Roger forced himself to ask.

Riordon said: 'Keep quiet.' He appeared to be listening intently, while the tune went on, not gathering in volume but still seeming to come from a long way off. Then it faded, and Riordon ran a hand through his thick, greying hair. 'I haven't much time,' he said harshly. 'West, where is that map?'

The reaction to that after the tune and the brief period of confidence was such that Roger just gaped at him. He hardly realised the full implications of the question. Then without warning Riordon stepped across the room and struck the side of Roger's face with the palm of his hand. The blow stung, and sent Roger reeling backwards in the chair.

'Where's the map?' Riordon demanded. He stood with his hands clenched, as if ready to deliver another blow, and Roger could hear his heavy breathing.

Roger said with an effort: 'Don't do that again.'

'I will strangle the life out of you unless you tell me where the map is!' shouted Riordon. He seemed quite mad, the glitter in his eyes held a fanatical glint. He curved his hands and put them about Roger's throat, beginning to squeeze until the breath came with difficulty through Roger's windpipe. 'Tell me what you've done with it, tell me where it is!'

Roger brought his right knee up into Riordon's stomach.

Riordon was standing in such a position that the full force of the blow struck against the pit of his stomach, but for a split second Roger wondered whether he would find the same steel protection as Mark had done. But the blow went home, and Riordon gasped and staggered back, taking his hands away. Roger jumped to his feet to follow up his advantage, knew that Riordon could not help himself for minutes to come, and was filled with a fierce exhilaration. Then something dropped over his head.

It was a piece of cloth, and he saw it as he glanced swiftly upwards. He raised a hand to try to push it away, and half-turned. He caught a glimpse of a tiny creature, no more than two feet high, *standing on the back of his chair:* then the cloth was forced over his face and drawn tightly about his neck.

Of Lionel Michison

IT WAS very dark.

The cords or strings about Roger's neck were drawn tightly but not enough to threaten to strangle him. His wrists were bound, but not tightly, and he did not think that his assailant had intended the bonds to be permanent. The sacking, or whatever it was over his eyes, smelt faintly musty. It admitted no light.

He knew that he was still stretched on the floor of Michison's lounge. He remembered vividly his single glimpse of the dwarf, and could recall how, when he had been knocked off his balance, he had felt the creature's tiny feet stepping over him. He could recall, too, the touch of very cold, tiny fingers at his wrists.

Then there had been a sudden silence: one moment the cords had been tightened about him, the next that silence, broken after a few seconds by a sound on the stairs – or that was what he had thought for it had been like hurried footsteps and there had been a hollow, echoing note.

It seemed a long time since then, but he knew that he had been on the floor only a few minutes. The suddenness of the attack had dazed him, and his head was swimming; he did not realise that it was partly due to the earlier blow on the head and the resounding slap from Riordon. Nor did he know whether to be relieved or alarmed; he came to the conclusion that there was nothing at all normal about Riordon, nothing he expected of the man materialised. He had a vague impression that

Riordon had been alarmed when the *Concerto* had been played a few minutes before; that was reassuring.

The *Concerto* had been played by the little dwarf, of course.

That explained so many things, making it easy to understand how the dwarf could slip into houses without being seen, how he could keep watch for the police and warn Riordon when they were approaching. One uncanny element was explained, anyhow.

'Damn it, what am I doing?' Roger muttered suddenly.

He began to work at the cords about his wrists. He was not surprised that they came off with little trouble, but when he began to try to untie the knot at the back of his neck he found it much more difficult. He was sitting up and working at it when he heard another sound.

A door was opening.

There followed a soft *click,* and he imagined a slight lessening of the darkness. Faint footsteps sounded above the beating of his heart, and then another *click,* as of an electric light switch being pressed down.

'*Oh!*' gasped a woman.

Roger could not see her, but the light from the lamp crept up from his neck and came through the cloth about his head. He tried to speak, but managed only a muffled voice and words which were not clear even to himself. He heard another gasp, and then: 'Lionel. *Lionel!*'

Roger thought vaguely: 'Lionel? She can't mean Michison!'

'Hallo,' came a deep and reassuring man's voice. 'What's the trouble, Fluff?' More footsteps, heavy but muffled, sounded outside, and then the speaker broke off abruptly. After a pause he went on in a slow voice: 'Well I'm damned!' Another pause: 'It looks as if he's been strangled with his own mask! Stay there, Fluff.'

The voice, thought Roger absurdly, was as familiar as that of a close friend's; it was Michison's. He could imagine the man announcing the next item, an incomparable compère with just the right 'between you and me' friendliness in his voice. Then he sensed a movement nearer him, and Michison went on: 'I'll unfasten that. Don't you try to.'

Roger said nothing, and the knot was untied after Michison's nails had scratched the nape of his neck painfully. When the cloth was drawn from his head Roger closed his eyes against the bright light, catching only a glimpse of a pair of small woman's shoes a few feet away from him.

'Get up,' said Michison.

Roger kept his eyes closed and stood up, putting out a hand to steady himself against the chair. He opened his eyes; they watered and were filled with dust. So were his mouth and nose. He took out a handkerchief and blew his nose vigorously, took a corner of the handkerchief and wiped his eyes. Gradually things took shape: Michison was standing only a couple of yards from him, frowning and with one hand clenched and half-raised. 'Fluff', the original of the photograph on the mantelpiece, was standing by the open door with a hand resting against it. She gave the impression of being prepared to dash away at the slightest alarm.

Roger licked his lips and said: 'There's another one of us, I think.'

'Oh,' said Michison, and scowled more heavily. 'You're a humorist, are you?'

'No,' said Roger. 'But I'm dying of thirst.' He took out his wallet, and was relieved to find his official cards still inside. He selected one and handed it to Michison, saying: 'It might be hard to believe, but that's me. Could there be a drink? Preferably water?' He looked about the room for anything to quench his appalling thirst, while Michison said in incredulous tones: 'Chief Inspector *West!*'

'Yes,' said Roger. 'Look here—'

'Fluff, get him some water, will you?' asked Michison slowly.

Roger, who had always believed that Michison was a pleasant fellow, and well worth knowing, grew convinced that the conception had not been false. The girl moved away quickly, after only a moment of hesitation, returning in a few seconds carrying a glass of water; some of it spilled over the edge of the glass, for her hand was unsteady.

'There you are,' she said in a weak voice. She was pretty and very feminine, the light waving hair about her head explaining her nickname.

'Thanks.' Roger swilled a little water round his mouth before swallowing, then took a deeper drink. It was cold and refreshing, and he drew a deep breath when the glass was empty. His head was clearer and he was faintly amused at Michison's puzzled stare and the understandable apprehension of 'Fluff'. But there were other matters, some even more important than the astonishing appearance of Michison, whom Riordon claimed to have put away.

'Look here, I can explain fully,' said Roger, 'but first we ought to look round. When I came here I had a sergeant with me.' He did not explain how Sloan had disappeared, and saw 'Fluff's' lips widen in a silent gasp. 'What other rooms are there?'

'Fluff, stay here,' said Michison.

He looked very like his photograph as he treated Roger to a prolonged stare, and then led the way into the lounge hall. There were five doors leading from it, all painted black with red lines, and he opened the nearest, looking inside a tiny dining room, empty but for furniture. He tried a bedroom with the same result, but when he opened the third door, leading to another bedroom, he drew a sharp breath.

Looking over the man's shoulder, Roger saw Sloan.

The sergeant was laying on his side. His knees were doubled up, his arms held over his head. The side of his head was covered with blood which had seeped onto the carpet, and for a moment Roger thought that he was dead.

In that brief moment he saw a picture of Crummy Parker in his mind's eye: the wound in Sloan's head was almost identical with that from which Parker had died.

During the next few minutes Roger warmed still more to Lionel Michison.

The man turned, said something to Fluff, presumably to reassure her, and then rejoined Roger, who was on one knee beside Sloan's outstretched body. Now that he was nearer Roger could see that Sloan was breathing, and when he felt the sergeant's pulse it seemed fairly strong. The wound was ugly, and a closer inspection made Roger even more certain that it was like Parker's; probably it had been caused by the same, or a similar, instrument.

'My wife's calling a doctor,' Michison said.

'Oh, good. I think he'll get over this packet,' said Roger, straightening up. 'I wonder if there could be some warm water, and the usual stuff?' He lit a cigarette as he spoke, then bent down and put Sloan into a more comfortable position before making a more closer examination of the wound. His belief that the wound in Parker's head had been virtually the same was further strengthened.

By the time the doctor had arrived the wound was cleansed, and looked much less gruesome, while Roger had telephoned the Yard for an ambulance, photographers and fingerprint men, and had washed away the dust from the piece of coarse sacking which had been over his head.

The usual formalities were necessary, even though Michison would probably feel rueful about it, and there seemed little need for further evidence that Riordon had made the attack. Michison heard him talking on the telephone, and Fluff stood nearby regarding Roger curiously with her great eyes. When he had replaced the receiver, Michison grimaced and said slowly: 'You couldn't avoid your usual performances, I suppose?'

'I'm afraid not,' said Roger apologetically. 'But I'll guarantee that none of the men do any damage to the flat, and they'll leave it as they found it. Meanwhile—' he smiled a little although by no means certain how Michison would react to what he had to say – 'something in the way of an explanation is necessary, isn't it? What took you out tonight, when you knew I was coming?'

'I knew what?' asked Michison blankly.

Roger stared: 'Are you going to tell me that you didn't know that I was due to see you at nine-fifteen?'

'I hadn't the faintest idea,' Michison assured him warmly. 'I couldn't have done, anyhow. We've been visiting my wife's family all the afternoon, and arrived back only a short while ago. When you heard us,' he added. 'Now just what is this about? I had a sergeant asking me about a man named Riordon a couple of days ago, the fellow seemed to think that I knew him. Is this connected with the same business?'

'It is,' said Roger grimly, and hardly recovered from his surprise. 'Sloan – the injured sergeant – telephoned here for an appointment earlier in the evening. Someone made it for you.'

'Look here, darling,' said Fluff Michison quietly, 'I'm only in the way, and you can tell me all about it later. I can see the Inspector is going to ask you questions but doesn't like to because I'm here, and I promised to go downstairs and see Mabel as soon as we came back. Will that be all right?' she added, smiling at Roger.

'You won't leave the building, will you?'

'No.' She sounded dubious. 'Is there any reason why I shouldn't?'

'I'd prefer it if you didn't.'

'Well, I always like to make everyone happy,' said Fluff. 'Don't make Lionel promise not to tell me what it's all about. He won't keep the promise, so it would be a waste of time. How long will you be with him?'

'About half an hour,' said Roger.

'Now that you've managed to dissect me between you, I'll put a word in,' said Michison drily. 'Mabel can wait, Fluff. You may as well hear what West has to say, and it'll save me going over it again.'

'Oh, well, if you *really* insist.' Fluff was obviously delighted. Before Roger could start, however, the ambulance and another sergeant from the Yard arrived. Roger gave the man brief instructions, leaving him after the doctor had given orders to the ambulance driver and the stewards. The confusion at the flat died away quite soon, although there were occasional noises when the photographers and fingerprint men entered and began their work.

Roger was intrigued by the calm way in which the Michisons took the intrusions. He even wondered if they were not a little too calm, but preferred to think that they were adept at accepting things as they came. Fluff's manner, light-hearted, and so reminiscent of Janet's, was natural enough, and Michison gave the impression of being puzzled but not perturbed; that too was natural. The fact that he knew the police were interested in him probably explained something of the calmness with which he accepted the invasion of the flat.

Roger spoke when they were all sitting in the modern easy chairs. 'I'll be as brief as I can,' he said. 'I understand that the man Riordon, who is wanted by us for several reasons, came to Broadcasting House to see you two days ago. Or three days,' he added, realising that he was not quite certain of his facts.

Michison shook his head slowly. 'He didn't.'

Roger said: 'No one having once seen him could forget Riordon.' He gave a brief word picture, watching the others closely all the time, but except that Fluff made a moue once or twice they showed no expression. Towards the end of his recital he had an uncomfortable feeling that Michison was right and that Riordon had not been to see him. Yet the evidence that Riordon had entered his room came from a reliable police officer, as a result of the interrogation of lesser officials at Broadcasting House.

'I'll admit I wouldn't have forgotten that fellow if he came to see me,' said Michison. 'But as I told your sergeant no one came to my office that evening. I'd given orders that I wasn't to be disturbed unless it was something of exceptional importance, you see. I was working on a script needed the next morning,' he added with a smile, 'and it had to be ready in time. I'm afraid you've been misinformed.'

'Apparently,' said Roger heavily.

'Aren't policemen lucky?' demanded Fluff in dulcet tones. 'If anyone else said anything like that Lionel would punch him on the nose for calling him a liar.'

Involuntarily Roger smiled. 'He's a nicer appreciation of the situation, I hope! I've been battered about quite enough tonight. Well, now . . .'

He told them again of the interview which Sloan had arranged, and the inescapable evidence that someone had been at the flat to take the message. Moreover Riordon and the little dwarf (whom he did not mention) had undoubtedly been in possession and made themselves completely at home.

At that juncture, Fluff interrupted: 'Darling, I haven't looked in my jewel case.'

'I don't think Riordon is that kind of visitor,' said Roger.

Fluff was not satisfied, however, until the three of them had been in the main bedroom, unlocked a drawer of the dressing table, and examined some small oddments of jewellery, all untouched. Fluff fingered them with relief. 'They're not exactly the Crown Jewels,' she said, 'but I'm rather fond of them.' She put them back, locked the box and then relocked the drawer, and led the way back to the lounge.

'I wonder why Riordon had chosen me for his particular kind of joke,' Michison said. 'What sort of a customer is he?'

Roger said: 'Not nice in any way.'

'I'd gathered that, but—' Michison broke off. 'There isn't a lot I can do about it, but I wish I knew the beggar who told you that he'd been to see me. He might have been at Broadcasting House, of course, and someone may have mistaken the room he went into. Er – had he any right to be there? I mean, had he a pass or anything like that?'

'Not to my knowledge.'

'Then he must have had an acquaintance there,' said Michison. 'Getting inside is like getting into a holy of holies, but somewhat more rigid. You don't think he's likely to trouble us again, do you?'

Roger said quickly: 'I'd say he's done all he wants to do here. And I hope my fellows have, too.'

He went out, to find that the men from the Yard had finished their work and had made a fairly good job of cleaning the carpet where it had been stained with Sloan's blood.

Roger saw them off the premises, and then returned to the lounge.

He could not help feeling that there was something at the flat which would help him, if he could only discover what it was. The evidence that Riordon had not seen Michison whoever else he had visited at Broadcasting House, confused the trails far more effectively than anything else had done, and he found Michison's story convincing. There was no reliable evidence, now, that either Morris at the Admiralty or Bennett at the Home Office were implicated.

'It looks as if all I have to do now is to say "sorry", and add thanks for the way you've taken the intrusion.' Roger smiled apologetically. 'Except – there's just a chance that you might find out for me whom Riordon did visit. I'd prefer the inquiries to be discreet, and you may not feel like making them.'

'I've no objection,' said Michison, 'especially if it's helping you people. I propose to find out who put you on to me, in any case. It's no use asking you to give me the name of your informant, I suppose?'

'Offhand, I can't tell you,' said Roger truthfully. 'But if you will make a few discreet inquiries I'll be grateful. Oh, by the way – do you know the man who broadcasts on the harmonica occasionally?'

Michison stared: 'What on earth has that got to do with it?'

'Riordon's signature tune is played on the instrument,' said Roger, and stepped to the radiogram unexpectedly. 'Do you mind?' He raised the lid, and saw that a record was in place; he read the little paper disc stuck to it. It was the right record, for it said: '*Warsaw Concerto – Reggie Bright – Harmonica*'.

He switched on and put the needle into position; neither of the Michisons moved, but stared towards him in bewilderment. The tune began very softly but increasing in volume, carrying with it a queer, almost nostalgic memory. Roger stood listening with compressed lips, until startled by a ring at the front door bell.

'Oh damn!' said Fluff, who was on the far side of the room. She opened the door, and, after a pause and a mutter of voices, called out: 'It's a man who says he wants to see you, Inspector.'

Roger went quickly towards the open door, wondering who had come back and assuming that it was one of the men from the Yard, when an explosion came. It was not deafening but loud enough to make him jump; and he felt the blast from it. He staggered against the wall, then turned in time to see Michison falling to the floor, smoke pouring from the radiogram and a few red stabs of flame shooting up amongst it. Pieces of the records were flying about the room, some of them in flames.

News of Marion Byrne

ROGER WENT forward as soon as he regained his balance, to see Michison gasping, his face twisted in pain. Roger raised his voice to summon the man from the door, and Fluff appeared. She said nothing but flew towards the two men.

'Get a fire extinguisher,' Roger called.

The smell of burning in the room was growing pungent, and the pile of the carpet was alight in several places, each outbreak sending up a little wisp of smoke and stab of flame. Roger eased Michison up and half-carried, half-dragged him out of the room. Fluff was tense-faced but self-possessed. She told a plain-clothes man who put in a startled appearance where to find a fire extinguisher. Leaving Michison in an easy chair doubled up, gasping, and with a cut on his forehead which was bleeding freely, Roger hurried to the landing for the extinguisher.

By then the plain-clothes man, one of the fingerprint experts, began using another; an evil-smelling chemical from it filled the flat.

Gradually they subdued the flames.

The fire had not been serious, although had the action been less prompt, had the only people in the flat been injured by the explosion, there would have been little chance of saving the contents of the room, while the whole flat might have been gutted. As it was, twenty minutes later there was only the smell of smoke, little pools of water, and a drenched carpet, a few slightly damaged chairs, and the wreckage of the radiogram.

The top part of it had been blown out, and the wood of the case split and twisted by the flames.

Michison had been struck in the stomach by a piece of debris, but had suffered no other injury beyond the scratch on his forehead. About the walls of the lounge gramophone needles were sticking out, blown there by the blast. To Roger this freak effect had much in common with the whole affair. He could see no sense in it, could not understand why it had been necessary, unless Riordon had expected him to be standing near the instrument at the moment of the explosion.

Even then there was no certainty that the eruption would have killed him, and had Riordon wanted him dead he would surely have chosen a more reliable method, so that Roger could not have defended himself.

He arranged for a police guard at the flat, assured himself that the Michisons were not unduly perturbed, and went back to the Yard. On the way, driving Sloan's car and with the fingerprint man alongside him, he felt a heavy sense of depression.

He considered that there was cause for it.

He had left for three interviews, from none of which had he expected much information, but all of which might have helped him to fit some pieces into the puzzle. He had left the Yard with Sloan as buoyant and confident as he himself; and Sloan, even if he did not succumb to his injuries, would be off duty for months and might not fully recover from the effect of the attack.

The Michison angle had led him to a further confusion of trails, too. There seemed no purpose in what Riordon had done, but the man was not one to act purposelessly; it had all been carefully calculated to cause a required effect; Roger's anxiety to find out just what the effect was had probably been foreseen.

'Why did you come back, Thomas?' he asked his driver suddenly.

'I left some of my kit behind, sir, and wasn't *quite* sure

whether you wanted me to get prints of the lady and gentleman there. I thought I'd better have a word with you about that.'

'I see,' said Roger.

The remarks set him wondering whether the Michisons were as innocent as they appeared; their cool acceptance of abnormal conditions was praiseworthy in one way, but it might well be suspicious. He was more than a little suspicious of people whose background appeared quite innocent, and who had no apparent motive for the crime, nor any known association with Riordon.

There was one possibility which worried him. Riordon had made a great ado about getting the map.

Roger started: the man had asked him where it was that evening, making out that he had not got it. *Was* it possible that the map had been taken from Chatsworth by someone working against Riordon but *not* with the police?

It was just possible, Roger admitted grudgingly, but he disliked the thought that there were any factions of this affair unknown to the police.

There was another possibility.

Riordon might be making the play about the map to confuse the issues. He had 'led them' to Michison and the men at the Admiralty and the Home Office, but there was nothing to support the contention that he had interviewed Michison, and the same would probably apply to the other men. Those men, thought Roger gloomily, had been waiting up for him to visit them: Riordon could not have been at all three places, and there was reason enough to believe that he had left the sailor and the Home Office official alone for that night.

Had they telephoned to tell Riordon of the appointments?

Roger drew a deep breath.

The so-far unknown Morris and Bennett might have told Riordon of the interviews, but Michison could not have done had he been out of London until nearly ten o'clock. But if Michison had not passed on the message, if he had not taken Sloan's call from the Yard, how had Riordon ever guessed that

Roger would be making the calls at all?

He had been blinding himself, taking it for granted that Riordon had taken the call, because he had been in possession of the Michison flat all the evening: *why should he have been there if he were not associated with Michison?*

'I don't know whether I'm making mountains out of molehills or not,' Roger confided to himself. 'I do know I'm getting a headache.'

Headache or not, he was very active when he returned to the Yard. He sent men to the flats of Commander Morris and Sir William Bennett respectively, with instructions to watch them throughout the night and to find out whether either of them had had callers the previous evening. Routine precautions were already being taken, and a complete dossier on the two men would be available in the morning.

He put into motion further inquiries about Reggie Bright, of harmonica repute, and called for the names and addresses of circus proprietors and theatrical agents, all of whom might put him in touch with someone who knew a dwarf who was also adept on the harmonica. The one consolation of the night's misadventures was that he had seen the dwarf, and thus understood how Riordon managed to get the *Warsaw Concerto* warning. It was simple, thought Roger, concentrating on the good facet of news and feeling his depression lifting. It might even be possible for the dwarf to get into the Yard; he could have been in Sloan's room when Sloan had made those appointments.

'At least the uncanny element has gone,' Roger reassured himself, rubbing his tired eyes. 'If I don't get some sleep soon I shall feel as bad as ever in the morning.' He yawned, stood up, and then went downstairs to the basement, where one large room was used as a dormitory for men who needed to stay at the Yard overnight. There were partitions which gave some privacy, and Roger kept a spare set of pyjamas, a toothbrush and other toilet accessories there. He had brushed his teeth, washed, and was changing into pyjamas when another question flashed across his mind.

The dwarf had been inside the room: how had he known that the Michisons had been on the way up the stairs?

'My God!' thought Roger. 'And I said it was no longer uncanny!'

His depression grew deeper when the corollary to the question, one which he should have seen much earlier, occurred to him. Why had Riordon been so anxious to avoid the Michisons? Surely he could have handled them as easily as he had Roger?

Roger could not settle for sleep until he had gone upstairs again and sent two detective constables to strengthen the watch which he had set outside the Michisons' house. He determined that his first inquiry the next morning would be into that charming compère and his vivacious wife.

As he was between waking and sleeping he thought guiltily that he had spared hardly a thought for Janet since he had left Hinton Magna.

About the time that Roger and Sloan walked up the stairs of the dingy house near Portland Place, Paula Dean leaned across Janet, and switched off the radio; there was a talk by a dreary-voiced professor, who faded abruptly.

Paula tucked in loose strands of auburn hair, and said sharply: 'If you two weren't bad enough, *he* would have driven me crazy. Mark, I *know* Marion will turn up, nothing happens to a girl like Marion. It stands to reason.'

'Does it?' asked Mark, and tried to smile. 'If I had more time, I'd work out the logic of that, but just now it would be too much for me. I wonder how Roger's getting on?'

At that moment the phone rang and Janet dashed to answer it. Her voice came clearly from the hall.

'Who?' she said, and paused. 'Who? No, I'm sorry, I can't hear you very well. Yes, please, spell it.' There was another pause, and then the first letter came. 'M,' she called, 'A – R –

I—' then she broke off abruptly, and shouted: 'Mark, come quickly! Yes, yes, I can hear you, Marion – Mark, come on!'

Mark was already on his feet and moving towards the door when Paula, two yards away from him, raised her voice and shouted: 'Mark, it's Marion. Hurry!'

Janet's eyes were glistening as she held the receiver towards Mark and spoke into the mouthpiece. 'Yes, he's just coming but I can't hear you very well – here he is, hold on.' In a lower voice to Mark, she added: 'She's very faint, but she seems to be hearing me all right.'

'Bless you,' murmured Mark, and took the receiver. 'Hallo,' he said, in a low-pitched voice, speaking close to the telephone. 'Is that all right?' He paused. 'Good, yes, I can hear you clearly, my darling.' That slipped out so casually that Janet hardly noticed it. 'Where did you say? Reading – yes, I heard all right, Woodhill, near Reading, yes – but are you all right?' He paused again, and Paula came into the hall, putting an arm about Janet's waist and staring at Mark as keenly as Janet. 'You're sure?' said Mark. He listened for some minutes. 'Well, it takes some believing – no, I mean understanding! Of course I believe you . . . what? . . . you stay there, and don't move out of that pub. Someone will be along during the night or early in the morning, just stay put. You've really had me scared! Yes, scared!' He laughed again, as if light-heartedly. 'Yes, first thing – what's the number? . . . Woodhill 35. Yes, if I can't get there myself I'll telephone early in the morning. All right, Marion, goodbye for now.'

He held the receiver in his hand for a few moments, then slowly replaced it. He rubbed the back of his neck when his hand was free, and looked at the others as if he did not know that they were near. An explosive 'Well?' from Paula made him start and widen his eyes.

Janet saw a peculiar thing: the smile which he had shown when he had talked to Marion had grown set: it was not a reflection of relief or of pleasure; the smile was very nearly tense, as if he did not feel as happy at hearing from her as he might have done.

'Well, what did she *say?*' demanded Paula impatiently. 'Mark, you *are* impossible.'

'Yes, aren't I?' said Mark slowly. 'It's a queer story. I'd better put a call into Roger straight away. Where do you think I'm likely to get him?'

'He'll sleep at the Yard,' said Janet confidently.

Mark put a call through to Whitehall 1212, was told that there was up to an hour's delay, and failed to convince the operator or the supervisor that the call should have priority. He was tempted to make contact with the Dorchester police and to ask them to telephone the Yard, but was anxious to explain to Roger exactly what Marion had told him. So he put up with the unavoidable delay, and returned to the lounge, while Paula declared in clear undertones that some people had no consideration for anyone. And: 'What *did* happen to her, Mark?'

'She doesn't know.'

'What!' exclaimed Janet and Paula, as in one voice.

'She *says* that she doesn't know, I mean,' corrected Mark. 'She came to the cottage for her handbag and found it on a seat in the loggia, and then she went back to the Manor. While walking through the grounds she saw the tramp, and she went a long way round to try to avoid him. And then—' Mark drew a deep breath and rubbed the back of his head again – 'then someone came out of the copse near where she was walking, and all she remembers is feeling a sharp pain in her arm.'

'Mark!' gasped Paula. 'It couldn't have been just like that!'

'Why not?' asked Mark. His smile had grown set. Against his inclination he must have seen the possibility that Marion's story was not true. 'There are drugs which can send you to sleep in a few seconds,' he added, 'including one or two in regular use today. Regular medical use, I mean.'

'But what happened afterwards?' demanded Paula.

'Marion says she came round this afternoon, finding herself in a country district which she didn't recognise,' replied Mark.

'She had her handbag with her, and her money hadn't been touched. She walked for an hour or more, and then managed to get a lift into the nearest village, a place called Woodhill. It's on the Newbury side of Reading. She was famished; and needed a wash, and stopped at the pub in the village, where she had some food and a bath. And then—' again he paused, and Janet imagined that this was the part which puzzled him most. 'She fell asleep. She didn't wake up until about half an hour ago, then she put in the call. I wish the Yard would come through,' he added irritably.

'What are you going to do, Mark?' asked Janet, bringing the conversation back to a more practical plane.

'I promised I'd phone Roger before doing anything on my own,' said Mark.

Then the London call came through – but proved an anticlimax. Inspector West was not in but was expected back soon. Disappointed and dissatisfied, Mark left a message for Roger to ring him back, and then telephoned the private number of Cartwright, the Dorchester Inspector. Cartwright had not gone to bed, and he listened to the story carefully, making notes and asking for occasional sentences to be repeated. When Mark had finished, Cartwright said: 'What have you in mind, Mr Lessing?'

'Nothing very much,' said Mark. 'I think it would be a good idea to get in touch with your Reading people, and ask them to send a couple of men to watch the hotel in Woodhill. We don't want anything else to happen to Miss Byrne.'

'I'll do that,' promised Cartwright. 'I'll ring through right away. Anything else, Mr Lessing?'

'Not now, thanks,' said Mark.

It was a thoroughly unsatisfactory situation, and was not improved by a long wait for Roger's call. At half-past twelve the two girls went to bed, Paula declaring that she felt nervous and that she would like Janet to sleep with her. Mark was determined to wait until a call came through from London, but the last sound he remembered was the dining room clock striking the hour of two.

When he awakened it was with a start and a puzzled glance about the room. The door was ajar, and light was coming through it, while there was an edging of daylight at the windows. He felt stiff and cramped, and grunted in disgust when he realised that he had fallen asleep in the easy chair. He wondered what had disturbed him, then heard footsteps somewhere in the house.

His lips tightened, and he got up from the chair, only to collapse again as pins and needles struck his legs. He kept pushing his legs outwards to ease the nerves, but the pain continued. The noise of someone moving about was unmistakable. He thought of Riordon, told himself that he was a fool, then heard a muttering voice. It was low-pitched and seemed to come from a long distance off; undoubtedly it was a man's. It continued for a long time, until he was able to move freely. He looked about the room, picked up a poker, and crept towards the door.

Footsteps came from the kitchen, and he saw who it was.

Quickly, Mark withdrew into the dining room, grinning ruefully at the unnecessary alarm. It was the little servant, and he remembered Paula telling him that she liked to start work at half-past six so that she could be free all the afternoon. The voice was that of a BBC announcer giving a foreign broadcast.

'But confound it,' he said abruptly. 'Roger hasn't been through or I would have heard the telephone.'

He waited until the maid had returned to the kitchen, then went upstairs. A quick shower refreshed him. He found that he was able to use his right hand much more freely than had been possible for some days past. He had to wait until after the girl had brought up some tea before he had any shaving water, but was shaved and feeling much better before either Janet or Paula left their room. Janet was anxious to know whether Roger had been through.

'No,' said Mark. 'I'll ring him about eight.'

'He couldn't have had your message,' said Janet. 'I hope—'

she broke off abruptly.

Mark needed no telling that she was thinking that Roger might not have returned to the Yard at all. Mark went to take a turn round the orchard before breakfast, and he was some distance from the house when he heard a faint sound, different from the flitting of the birds, the distant noise of a plough, or the even beat of an aeroplane engine high in the sky. It came from close at hand.

He looked about him, and could see nothing, although he was filled with vague alarm. The noise was repeated several times, and for the life of him he could not prevent himself from thinking that it sounded like a quick blast on a mouth organ. The refrain of the *Warsaw Concerto* passed through his mind several times, and when eventually the tune did come softly towards him from the trees, he was uncertain whether it was real or whether it sprang from autosuggestion. His uncertainty faded; the tune was unmistakable, and it came from above his head.

He looked upwards, his heart beating fast, and moved towards a gnarled apple tree, scores of years old, subconsciously feeling that he could get more cover from it. The tune persisted, although he knew that it would not be heard at the house; it was almost as if this rendering was for his especial benefit. He told himself that he would not have minded so much had it come from the ground, but it was being played amongst the branches of a tree which had branches almost touching the ground, an old favourite which Paula refused to have pruned.

Then he saw a grotesque little creature, no more than two feet tall, standing on one of the branches. The dwarf was holding a mouth organ with two tiny hands, and the instrument poked out either side of his face like a monstrous clipped moustache.

The tune went on and on.

Mark Lessing and the Dwarf

MARK DID NOT look away from the creature in the trees.

After the first shock he realised that, unexpected though it was, there was nothing particularly scarifying in the sight of a dwarf. Nor was there the slightest hint that the little man threatened danger, except that tune which went on and on as if it had no end. The mouth organ moved from side to side, the tiny, well-shaped hands seemed overburdened with it.

As his heart grew steadier, Mark studied the dwarf.

He was certainly little more than two feet tall, dressed in lounge clothes which fitted him well but made him look unreal. His face was round and red, and the features were broad; he looked more like a ventriloquist's dummy than a human being. His hair was thin and grew well back on his head, had he been normal Mark would have judged him a man in the middle-forties.

Mark waited until at last the dwarf removed the harmonica from his mouth and tucked it away inside his coat. Then he looked down at Mark, with his head on one side. He balanced without the slightest difficulty on the frail tree branch.

After what seemed a long time, Mark said: 'Good morning.'

He had no time to reflect on the absurdity of the comment, for the dwarf smiled: that startled him.

'Good morning to you. You are Mr Lessing, Mr Mark Lessing.'

'That's right,' said Mark.

'I am glad to meet you,' said the dwarf. 'My name is

Richardson.' His voice was not deep but its tone was good and the words might have come from a man of normal size; true, the timbre was on a high pitch, but there was nothing else unusual in it. There was even a hint of mellowness. 'I nearly had that pleasure in Fulham, but I hurried away with Count Riordon.'

'Oh,' said Mark blankly.

'Of course you are surprised,' said the dwarf: he looked saddened, even troubled. 'Not only by my appearance here, but also by my admission that I am acquainted with Riordon. As a matter of fact I have worked for Riordon for many years; think it is almost true to say that he would be helpless without me. He has grown used to me and to my protection, and – as he takes so much – he now takes me for granted. Have you ever thought, Mr Lessing, that it is a mistake to take anyone for granted?'

Mark drew a deep breath. 'It's a favourite opinion of mine.'

'I am not surprised,' said the dwarf. 'Mr Lessing, I played the *Concerto* just now because I was anxious to attract your attention and to offer you something in the way of proof that I am associated with Riordon. You have no doubt about that, have you?'

'None – none at all,' said Mark with an effort.

'You do not sound very certain,' said the dwarf.

'I've no doubt,' Mark assured him more firmly.

'I am glad, because a great deal depends on your faith in me,' said the dwarf. 'I am talking to you because I believe that it will bring more results than if I talk to the police. I am an odd little creature, I know. I am a freak, and the trouble is that so many people are apt to look upon dwarfs just as that – as freaks whose minds are as diminutive as their bodies. It is not so, Mr Lessing. Our minds work on very similar lines to yours, and we have similar standards, similar hopes and ambitions. Like you, we fall in love, and, like you, we have our disappointments.'

Mark said: 'I don't doubt it.'

The dwarf paused, and Mark took his cigarette case from his

pocket, opened it, and proffered it. The dwarf leaned down, and with fingers little larger than the cigarettes themselves, took one and put it in his lips; it looked much as a very long cigar would look on a normal man. He accepted a light gravely, and kept the cigarette in his mouth.

Mark had wanted a few seconds to pull himself together, but the casual manner in which the dwarf who called himself Richardson took the cigarette prevented him from doing so. He felt quite out of his depth, and could not make his mind work evenly.

The dwarf said: 'Thank you. I have told you those few things, Mr Lessing, to make you understand what I am going to do more clearly. I will add a little. I listen to the wireless, just as you, and I read the newspapers. I have political opinions, like most people, and I know the difference between right and wrong. I am not very interested in that difference, and as I have worked for Riordon for a long time I must be classified as a criminal. In fact I have helped him with most of his crimes.'

Mark's throat felt dry, and he said nothing in the pause which followed.

Richardson went on: 'Perhaps I ought to explain even more fully. There are only a few dozen people of my stature in this country. We like to live together, or some of us do, but I have always been something of an adventurer on the modest scale on which dwarfs can become adventurers. And the theatrical business has never interested me. Posturing in front of ordinary people is nauseating! It is like an exhibition of nakedness in a Soho striptease club, but worse. It is making capital out of our misfortunes and our freakishness. I was on the stage for a short while and I grew to hate the people in the auditorium. Their titters, their so-called sympathy, their laughs – how would you like to be a subject of amusement, of ridicule, just because of a mischance in your selection of parents, if I may put it that way?'

'I shouldn't like it,' said Mark slowly.

'Of course you would not. And you can imagine, Mr Lessing,

that I grew to hate ordinary people. I mean *hate* them as I understand the word hate. I resented everything about them, their very normality, their huge, hideous, dull-witted faces, their cumbersome bodies. Oh, I hated them, Mr Lessing. Is it any wonder that I became antisocial?'

'No,' said Mark, with an effort.

'When I first met Riordon,' went on the dwarf, 'we were both in a mood of acute depression. My wife had died, and I was very lonely. And Riordon had a grudge against the world. All people who have grudges against the world become lonely, Mr Lessing: it is an invariable rule. I will not bore you with a history of our early association. I will tell you that Riordon was at first vastly amused by me, but there was a rough kindliness about the man which attracted me to him. It was soon evident, moreover, how easy it would be for me to hide myself in the houses of people whom he wished to victimise, and obtain information which led to blackmail. You can imagine that?'

'Yes,' said Mark stiffly.

'Don't imagine that I regret *that,*' said the dwarf in his level, matter-of-fact voice. 'Riordon rarely victimised the pure in heart, and those whom he blackmailed deserved their fleecing. I would have been quite happy to continue working with him, without any compunction whatsoever, but there were limits to the *degree* of the crimes which I would permit. It was not until a few days ago that I discovered the hideous fact that he is dealing with Russia, or with Russian agents, Mr Lessing.'

Mark drew a deep breath, and said: 'Go on.'

'Thank you.' Richardson inclined his head. 'I was shocked, but I did not reveal what I felt at first. I decided to ponder over it, and to try to find the easiest way in which to prevent Riordon from bringing his plans to full fruition. I have continued to work under his orders, and of course I am in a unique position to discover just what he is doing. I have not yet been admitted to his private counsels, but I can get into what he might call the council chamber whenever I wish. There is some degree of risk, just as there is some risk in approaching the police. I will admit that what I have seen of West I rather like. You see, I do not condemn every member of the community but form my own opinion. But I did not feel that I could tell the police, but I *could* tell you. You have advantages which West has not. You do not owe allegiance to any regulations or to any leader. You are able to take chances which West cannot, and I imagine that is one of the reasons why, between you, you have contrived to solve so many problems which the police themselves could not have done. So I make you an offer, Mr Lessing. I am prepared to tell you where to find Riordon's *real* headquarters.'

Mark said slowly: 'In return for what, Mr Richardson?'

Gently, almost sorrowfully, the dwarf shook his head. 'You do not really understand me, I see. I suppose that is asking too much. I am not making a deal with you, Mr Lessing. I want nothing in return for my confidences, except—' he paused for a moment, and threw the cigarette away: until then he had kept it between his lips. '*Except* your assurance that you will do everything in your power to prevent Riordon from succeeding in making further contact with Russia.'

'That goes without saying.'

'Good! I felt that, of course, but I wanted to make myself quite clear. Before I go on, I would like to ease your mind of one thing.' He gave a grotesque smile which made Mark's heart turn over. 'Concerning Miss Byrne. She did leave the Manor the other morning to come for her bag. I followed her, and I know. Riordon was here, or in the neighbourhood, and he told me to see what she was doing. Later I came here and took the map from Sir Guy's pocket. That astonishing, conceited creature asked for nothing else.'

Mark said quickly: 'Go on.'

'I knew that this news would make you much happier,' smiled the dwarf. 'And here are the other details. The tramp, Parker, was foolish enough to imagine that he could get the better of Riordon. No ordinary man can do that, Mr Lessing. At one time they were associated, and Parker imagined that he had been cheated by Riordon, so there was something of a feud between them. Riordon, who in many ways is a great man, brushed Parker aside much as you would a tiny insect. But Parker persisted. There is no doubt that he was going to try to bargain with you, offering you news of Riordon in return for money, but he did not know where Riordon had his headquarters. He had to find that out. He knew about me, of course, and thought that I would lead him to the place. He followed us here, and the only reason we came here in the first place was to find you and the map – you see, we thought you had it. Riordon, who is always prepared to look for new ways of increasing his income, learned that Colonel Byrne is a wealthy man and went to the Manor to try to find what he could amongst Byrne's papers – I had forced a way in, and admitted him; that has always been very easy. Unfortunately Parker knew that Riordon was inside, and went after him. It was very foolish of Parker. He went into the house by a door which Riordon had left open to make good his escape, and then came away a little later, not knowing that he had been seen.'

The dwarf paused but Mark made no comment. After several seconds the little creature went on: 'At the time I did not know what Riordon was really doing, Mr Lessing, and I was very loyal to him. Riordon and I staged a brief conversation, in which we talked of some money being in one of the rooms, an easy picking for a small-time thief but not tempting enough for him. They are Riordon's own words. He pretended to tell me just where the money was, and of course Parker could not resist the temptation to try to get it. He went in through the landing window. Riordon had gone back inside – he is not a man who refuses to take risks – and was waiting for Parker. He was standing by the wall, and struck Parker as he put his head through. It was over very quickly.'

Mark moistened his lips. 'It would have been,' he said.

'So, that explains Parker,' said the dwarf.

Mark said: 'And what of Miss Byrne?'

The dwarf said slowly: 'Riordon imagined that she would be an admirable hostage to coerce Colonel Byrne into cooperating, and so she was drugged – you have heard of evipan? The quick-acting narcotic drug? A remarkable discovery, and we have never had any difficulty in obtaining supplies. Riordon had a car waiting on the other side of the village, and Miss Byrne was taken away in that. It was on the way to London that Riordon made the first mistake I have ever known him make,' went on Richardson softly. 'He has a habit of talking to himself, and made a comment which made me wonder whether he was interested only in himself and making money. I took advantage of his confidence in me to look through some papers he was carrying in the car. They included the terms on which he is prepared to sell information about British secrets to the enemy. That was when I made up my mind to work *against* Riordon, although I decided that he was not to know it. He does not know it now.'

'I see,' said Mark.

'I thereupon played the *Concerto*,' went on the dwarf gently. 'I knew that it would worry him, and that he would think that the police were behind us. He took a side road – we were near Salisbury at the time – and then went on towards Reading. I will tell you in a moment where he has his headquarters. By then I had decided that you were my most likely confidant, and that I could best confide in you. Consequently I made suggestions which persuaded Riordon to leave Miss Byrne by the side of a country road, quite unhurt. I did that because I could hardly work against you in one way and with you in another. Moreover, I knew that you would want evidence of my sincerity. Doubtless you will hear from her, and she will corroborate my story.'

'She has,' said Mark slowly.

'Already? I am glad,' said the dwarf. 'It is always much better when there is mutual trust. And now, of course, you want the map. I have it. Riordon does not know that I have it, and *he* has a copy. The place which Riordon believes is quite safe from all suspicion is not far from Newbury, Mr Lessing, and you will be able to trace it quite easily from the map, which—'

He stopped abruptly, and looked away.

Mark, hearing a new sound, turned round to follow his gaze. Mark was so absorbed in what he had heard and what was promised that he did so with no feeling of alarm, only annoyance that the queer interview had been interrupted.

Then he caught a glimpse of Riordon storming through the trees.

The dwarf said in a harsh voice: 'He knows! I can see from his face. He knows!'

Then he turned and leapt higher up the tree, and as he did so the harmonica dropped from his coat and fell near Mark's feet.

Riordon Goes Wild

MARK DID NOT notice the instrument.

He saw Riordon's livid face and glaring eyes; and he knew that the dwarf was right. The man had overheard some of the conversation and probably guessed the rest. He was running with long strides, his right arm pushed forward with the hand clenched, and his left closer to his chest: in it he held a gun, dwarfed in his hand.

He fired twice, and the bullets lost themselves in the trees.

Mark ran for cover. There was no sense in flinging himself at Riordon, for he could not have stood a chance even with both hands free. He slipped behind the big apple tree, but Riordon appeared to have eyes for no one but the dwarf. He went blundering past Mark, and fired twice again. The noise of his progress drowned all other sounds except the sharp bark of the revolver shots; it was like the man to scorn using a silencer.

Someone shouted from the cottage.

Mark imagined that he saw the tiny figure of Richardson drop from a tree near the fence enclosing the orchard, on the far side, and scuttle along the road. Riordon might have seen him, also: in any case he stopped in his tracks and swung round towards Mark.

By then Mark had wrenched a small branch from a tree with his left hand. For a moment or two he would be safe from shooting behind the tree, although he did not like the odds against him. With any other man than Riordon he would have worried little about it either way, but the fear which Riordon contrived to create was strong within him. He searched the ground for stones, but there were none; not far away, however, were several small logs, dropped there when someone had taken an armful or a barrow-load across the orchard to the cottage. He bent down and retrieved two, flinging them at Riordon as the man approached. Riordon said: 'You damned fool, Lessing. You won't live another five minutes.'

He meant that: there was murder in his eyes. There was fear in Riordon, too, because Mark knew so much; and to Mark the most important thing seemed to be to save himself so that he could pass the information on.

The second log made Riordon sway to one side, and spoiled his aim. A bullet went past Mark and the tree, but was too close to be comfortable.

Mark flung the branch at the man.

He could not control his aim very well with his left hand, and took a chance of being shot while showing himself clearly: but Riordon sensed the danger and stepped to one side without shooting. The end of the branch touched his shoulder and pushed him to one side. Mark stepped back, putting more distance between himself and the man: and then he saw Janet at the edge of the orchard. Behind her was Paula, carrying a broom.

He shouted: 'Go away! Go away!'

He felt afraid of what would happen if Riordon turned upon them. He knew too much of the man's brute strength, knew that the girls would be helpless if they drew near. But neither of them heeded him, and Riordon came slowly towards him. Mark thought that there could not be more than two more bullets left in the gun. Once it was empty there would be a chance to escape.

Then men came running from the edge of the orchard.

They converged upon Riordon and Mark from all sides, five or six of them. Mark recognised two Yard men, and thought he saw dapper Cartwright from Dorchester. Two of the men were carrying heavy cudgels, and one carried an automatic. As

Riordon fired again the policeman with the gun pressed the trigger: both men missed.

Then Riordon realised his danger.

He swung round and flung the gun, obviously empty, at the man who bad fired at him; the speed with which he picked that fellow out as the most dangerous was astonishing. His aim was good and he caught the man on the side of the head, making him fall backwards. Then Riordon turned and ran – *towards Janet and Paula.*

Paula jumped away and made a sweeping blow with the broom. Riordon put up a hand and brushed it aside, then wrenched it from her hands. Holding the broom head, he swept the handle in front of him and caught Paula on the shoulder. The blow sent her toppling.

Janet ducked; the handle passed no more than a couple of inches above her head.

Riordon plunged on, again judging the weakest point in the cordon; only one man was directly ahead of him, after gaining several yards on the others. Riordon did not hesitate but went straight for the man, brushing aside a blow with a cudgel as if it had been with a feather. The next moment he sent the policeman staggering backwards with a blow from the broom.

The broomstick broke.

Riordon retained a part of it and went plunging on until he reached the fence. He leapt it without difficulty in spite of his limp. He landed in the road and then ran straight across and vaulted the hedge on the other side. As he sailed across, one of the policemen fired at him; the bullet went quite wide.

Mark could hear Riordon crashing through the undergrowth of the copse on the other side of the road, with the police streaming after him. Three of them leapt the orchard fence with nearly as much ease as Riordon, but the hedge on the other side baulked them. One stopped, and the other gave him a back. Even then he had to scramble over the hedge; probably he fell on the other side.

Mark drew a deep breath but did not join in the pursuit.

Instead he went quickly towards Paula and Janet. Paula was leaning against a plum tree and Janet was rubbing her cousin's shoulder, just where the blow had landed. Leaving them, Mark turned to the policeman who had taken the blow across the head.

The man was climbing unsteadily to his feet. The skin was broken, and there was blood on the side of his face. His gun had gone, and Mark assumed that one of his colleagues had picked it up and used it.

'Are you all right?' Mark asked unsteadily.

'Not too bad,' the man said, although he looked dazed. He added: 'God, that was a hell of a crack! He's got some strength.'

'You're telling me,' said Mark.

He led the policeman to the cottage, by the back door of which the little maid was standing with her lips parted and her eyes glistening: she looked less afraid than dumbfounded. But she was very good, for she led them promptly into the kitchen and started to prepare hot water and to get a towel and a sponge. When the kettle was boiling Janet and Paula arrived, Paula with the short sleeve of a shirt-blouse rolled up, and revealing a red weal already swollen and angry. She glared at Mark, and said: *'You* didn't do much.'

Mark swallowed hard. 'No,' he admitted. 'But I did all I could.'

'Pah!' snorted Paula. 'You just ran away from him.'

'Let's put some ointment on that arm of yours,' said Janet. 'Or would you rather let the doctor see it?'

'*I* want no doctor,' declared Paula.

Her disgust at Mark's safety first tactics remained evident for some time, and she gave him the impression that she had expected him to act something like Riordon. For his part, Mark was relieved that so little damage had been done and did not think that he had been wrong. He was glad when Janet and Cartwright, who came in soon afterwards, agreed that in the circumstances discretion had been wise. That was when they knew nothing of Richardson's story.

'But that brute got away,' Paula said stonily.

'Without leaving a trace I'm afraid,' Cartwright's voice was crisp. He smiled and he created a good impression. 'He had a motorcycle on the other road, and we had no chance to catch up. All the same, I think we got away with it very well. What caused it to start, Mr Lessing?'

Mark said slowly: 'One of his accomplices was talking about him.'

Cartwright's good-looking face reflected his surprise. 'Do you mean there was someone else in the orchard?'

'There was.'

'But I saw no one.'

'You wouldn't,' said Mark. 'He was—' he boggled at the word 'dwarf', and added after a pause: 'A small fellow, and able to slip in and out of the trees without being seen. He was there all right, and the quicker I see West about what happened the better it will be. I wish to heaven he'd given me that map before it happened.'

'The map?' Cartwright's manner made it obvious that he knew of the importance of the map. 'Did he talk about that?'

'Yes. And it's just possible he left it in the orchard. I think we ought to have a look round. Jan, will you have a word with Roger on the phone, and tell him that I'm coming up to town as quickly as I can get there? Tell him, too, that the place we're looking for is near Newbury. He can warn the Newbury people and can get inquiries started.'

'How do you know that?' asked Paula.

'A little bird whispered it in my ear, sweetie, and I thought I'd better live long enough to pass it on. I hope your conscience hurts you.'

'I have no idea what you mean,' said Paula indignantly.

Mark grimaced at her, then led the way into the garden and the orchard.

By then all of Cartwright's men and those from the Yard had returned, and they gathered about the old apple tree, all looking towards the ground. To Mark it seemed that there was, in fact, little point in the search, although he had suggested it. But he was rewarded in some measure, for half-hidden by the grass, was the mouth organ. He pointed it out, and a policeman retrieved it gladly.

'Be careful how you handle it,' said Cartwright sharply. 'It will need going over for prints.'

'I don't think there's a lot of need for that,' said Mark, taking out a handkerchief and stretching out a hand. 'Let me have a look at it, will you?' He took the instrument, one of normal size which was enamelled ornately: as harmonicas went it was undoubtedly a beauty. The 'keys' were covered with chromium or silver, and as he contemplated it he could imagine the *Warsaw Concerto* coming from it and causing so much apprehension and alarm.

'At least it won't be used to warn Riordon again,' he said abruptly. 'Cartwright, how quickly can you get me to London? The sooner I can have a talk with West, and he sees this and hears the rest of the story, the better it's going to be.'

Cartwright said: 'I've a car available any time. It's farther up the village. I'll drive you,' he added thoughtfully.

'Good man,' said Mark.

He would have started off without any delay, but Janet prevailed upon him to have some breakfast, which, she said, had been cooked a long time before and was being kept hot. She also discovered that Cartwright was hungry, and Paula, now in perfectly good temper, assured the Inspector that there was plenty for him and that she could even find a snack for his men. Cartwright assured her that they would not need it, but sat down with the others to a meal which Mark enjoyed despite the many things on his mind.

Janet had managed to speak to Roger.

He had received the message to telephone Mark, she had learned, only a few minutes before her call; the man who had taken it had been sent out on another job during the night, and had not passed it on until returning. Roger, said Janet, had made notes of all that she had to tell him, including the whereabouts of Marion Byrne, and had promised to take all the action possible. On hearing what had transpired at the cottage he had arranged for a general call to be sent out for Riordon: the limit of secrecy had been reached.

It was just after half-past nine when Mark and Cartwright started out for London. Mark thought that if the first half-hour's journey was any indication, they would get there in quick time, for Cartwright handled an MG with great skill.

As the journey went on he found himself thinking more and more about the map and the harmonica.

Soon after the call from the cottage, Roger went from his office to the canteen, breakfasted, and pondered over the case's more perplexing features. The confusion which the Michison business had caused had not sorted itself in any way during the night, and he felt that he was running against a series of brick walls. He had read the reports which had come in during the night, and none of them gave him assistance.

There was one on Commander Morris: it said that Morris had been at his flat the whole evening and during the night, as had Sir William Bennett of the Home Office. Roger hoped to be able to interview them himself before too long, but had to wait for Chatsworth, who had given express instructions for him to go to his office as soon as he arrived at the Yard.

The Michison reports helped little.

There was some conclusive evidence that Michison and 'Fluff' had been to Epsom, visiting 'Fluff's' parents, during the previous afternoon and early evening, and there was other evidence that the flat had been empty since noon on the previous day. The possibility that Michison was involved seemed slight indeed. Michison, moreover, had assured the police that there was no servant at the flat: the woman who had admitted Roger and Sloan had been one of Riordon's accomplices.

Had Riordon been there the whole evening, to take the message, Roger wondered? If not, how had he learned of it?

The thing worrying him most was that Riordon had known about the calls Sloan had put out. Certainly he had not gone to the flat to take the call, and had he known only about that one, Roger would have assumed that he had used Michison's place as a London rendezvous, probably to throw suspicion on the BBC man. But Riordon had known that he had telephoned both Morris and Bennett for appointments.

Roger telephoned both those men.

Morris was crisp and abrupt, although he did not give the impression that he had taken umbrage. He had arranged the interview, he admitted, and had waited in all the evening on the assumption that something unexpected had prevented the Inspector from calling at his flat. If it was of any use he promised to remain there during the morning, but said that he had an appointment of some importance during the early afternoon. Roger asked him to be good enough to remain at the flat until one o'clock.

Bennett of the Home Office was a different type: his voice boomed into the telephone, and he made it clear that he was extremely annoyed. He had already been worried by the police and told some fantastic stories, and he resented it very much because the appointment had been broken without any intimation reaching him. *Did* the police know what they were doing?

Roger apologised suitably, and persuaded Bennett that it would be helpful if he stayed in until twelve o'clock. After the talk with Chatsworth, Roger thought, then he could get the calls made.

Chatsworth telephoned for him just after ten o'clock.

The AC's face was very grave as he heard the various reports: he did not interrupt while Roger talked, and his first question afterwards was unexpected. 'How's young Sloan?'

'He's getting on, sir,' said Roger, who had telephoned the hospital. 'He's a bit delirious, I'm told, but there's no real danger. He should soon be able to tell us what happened.'

'H'm, yes,' said Chatsworth. 'But it isn't likely to add much to our store of knowledge, West. Nor is anything else.'

Roger demurred. 'We do know more, even if we can't understand it yet.'

'Oh, have it your own way,' said Chatsworth with acerbity. He lit a cigarette, dropped his match into an ashtray, and went on in a more relaxed voice. 'West, as I told you last night we mustn't let this case go on any longer.'

Roger said: 'We can only keep working, sir. Lessing might have something for us, and there is news of Marion Byrne.' He passed on that news.

Chatsworth nodded. '*If* Lessing is right, and the place is near Newbury, we may be getting somewhere. What else did you learn from him?'

'Not very much,' said Roger. 'I gathered that he thought it important to tell us the story first hand, and not to pass it on through anyone else. He should be here by three o'clock. I'm hoping for a lot from him.'

'Well, there's no harm in hoping,' said Chatsworth. 'Now what about this Michison business? And why do you think that radiogram was primed as a booby trap?'

'I can't for the life of me think of any good reason,' admitted Roger. 'They're both being watched.'

'So they should be. All right, go and see Morris and Bennett. And if Bennett is difficult, tell him that he ought to know better.'

Roger left the office.

When he reached the flat of Commander Morris he felt gloomy and pessimistic.

Morris was a short man, slim, grey-haired, with tired-looking pale grey eyes. His skin was dry, as if years at sea had taken the goodness from it; his thin face, with an almost lantern jaw, was relieved from grimness by full and humorous lips.

'Oh yes, Inspector West,' he said, rising from a hide armchair in front of a window overlooking St James' Park. 'Come in, Inspector.' He shook hands, his palm dry and cool. 'We haven't had the best of luck in meeting, have we?'

'It's good of you to take it like that,' said Roger.

'No other way to take it,' said Morris bluffly: his appearance was strangely at variance with his bluff manner, which had a kind of restrained heartiness. 'I've been wanting to see you as much as you've wanted to see me,' he added. 'About that fellow who was supposed to have visited me, I mean. I was told the name – Riordon, yes, Riordon.'

'Yes?' Roger said expectantly.

'I have made some inquiries,' went on Morris. 'I wormed an admission out of a man on my staff. A civilian named Banks.' Morris' expression gave his opinion of civilian assistants at the Admiralty. 'He *thought* he saw the man entering my office, and told your sergeant as much.'

'Isn't he sure now?' asked Roger with a faint smile.

Morris looked at him drily. 'He was never sure, and if I had my way I'd tan his hide. I talked to him late yesterday evening and told him to report to my office at nine o'clock this morning. I looked in,' added Morris. 'Banks didn't arrive. Funked it, obviously. I thought that might interest you, Inspector.'

'It certainly does. Have you his address by you?'

'Anticipated what you'd want,' said Morris with a smile. 'I've his file here.' He leaned forward and took a manilla folder from the top of a wireless cabinet, and from it extracted two slim cards. 'Here you are.'

Roger glanced at the cards, one of which gave the address of Arthur Banks as 41A, River Walk, Chelsea; his age as 24. There was also a photograph of an insipid-looking fellow with a weak mouth and doleful eyes: Banks was clean shaven, and his hair was dark. On the other card were particulars of his service at the Admiralty; he had been there for two years after being transferred from the Home Office.

Roger finished reading, and said: 'May I use your telephone?'

'Of course.'

Roger asked Eddie Day, who answered him at the Yard, to have a man go to see Banks and to take him to Cannon Row.

Then he thanked Morris and left the flat.

Outside he saw one of his men, on duty: he did not tell him that there was no further need to watch Morris, although he was inclined to doubt whether any useful purpose would be served by it.

Bennett was as different from Morris in appearance as he was in voice. A large, pompous man, dressed in a black coat and striped trousers, he made it clear that he resented police interference and that he would make a complaint in the necessary quarters. Roger was crisp and polite. He regretted the trouble, but said that the evidence that the man Riordon had visited the Home Office, and Bennett's room in particular, was very strong.

'Nonsense!' said Bennett. 'Never seen the man, and certainly I have no wish to. But now, Inspector, that you have gone to the trouble of coming to see me' – his sarcasm was laid on too heavily, thought Roger, the man was much too self-important – 'I would like to know *who* gave you the information.'

'A clerk in your Department, named Allen,' said Roger without reference to his notes.

Bennett stared. '*Allen?* Are you sure?'

'I am quite sure,' said Roger equably, but he wondered what had happened to disturb Bennett's equanimity. He did not like the way the man regarded him, nor the moment of hesitation, born of astonishment, which followed his assurance.

'Allen!' exclaimed Bennett. 'I can hardly believe that, Inspector. I found Allen a most careful and diligent assistant, and I was most grieved when I heard what had happened to him.'

Roger snapped: 'What has happened?'

'He met with a fatal accident on the Underground,' said Bennett slowly. 'My secretary telephoned me about it only an hour ago. Poor fellow, he was unlucky enough to slip as a train was coming into the station. At Piccadilly,' he added, and exuded a long, slow breath. 'Are you sure that it was Allen?'

'I'm even more sure that it was,' said Roger grimly.

There remained only the clerk who had 'reported' on Riordon's visit to Michison. By then Roger felt reasonably certain that Riordon had gone to a lot of trouble to draw suspicion on the three men, solely with a view of foxing the police. He could imagine Riordon's sardonic amusement at the success of the ruse. There was little doubt that he had persuaded, or bribed, Allen and Banks to give the false information, and the methods by which that had been contrived would be discovered eventually. He had little doubt that Allen had been murdered, and was afraid that Banks would not be found alive. Riordon was taking greater risks, was trying to cover up his traces while retaining his astonishing disregard for personal danger.

Roger telephoned Michison and asked him what he knew of a girl clerk named Groves: Amy Groves, said the report in his pocket, had testified to Riordon visiting Michison.

'That sweet child has been a pain in my neck for a long time,' said Michison in his pleasant voice. 'Why, what's she done?' He paused, and then added sharply: 'She didn't name me, did she? Is that what you're driving at?'

'Yes,' said Roger drily.

'The little vixen!' said Michison with feeling. 'She—er—it's a little difficult to explain, West, but some time ago she rather set her cap at me. D'you follow?'

'Didn't you like the angle?' asked Roger.

Michison chuckled, although he did not seem particularly amused. 'I can't say that I did. Groves took it rather badly – she's a pretty little piece, and she hadn't found men difficult before. We were always having trouble. In fact that script I was working on was lost by her, and I wondered whether there was any malice in it. To keep me grinding at the desk late, d'you follow?'

'I do,' said Roger. 'Where is she now?'

'She's taken the morning off,' said Michison. 'Someone telephoned for her this morning to say she had to go to the dentist to have a tooth out.' He paused. 'I suppose you'll want her address?'

'Have you got it?'

'It'll be in the files,' said Michison. 'Can I give you a ring later?'

'Please,' said Roger. 'I'll be at the Yard.'

He had called from a telephone kiosk, and was very thoughtful as he stepped from it. Riordon had covered himself well. Amy Groves, spiteful and conceited if he judged from Michison's comments, would not lead to Riordon any more than Allen or Banks. He wished he could understand why Riordon had gone to such trouble to draw those red herrings across his path, and walked slowly from Victoria Street towards the Yard.

There was nothing waiting for him, and he went for a snack lunch. At a quarter-past two he opened his office door, to hear Eddie Day saying: 'No, he's *not* . . . yes, I know, but . . . oh, wait a minute, here he is. This ruddy telephone,' Eddie added sotto voce as Roger took it from him. 'It's always ringing for you.'

'Good,' said Roger, and set Eddie chuntering in annoyance. 'It's Inspector West speaking.'

'It's Smithson speaking, sir, from Chelsea.' It was a man who had gone to check up on Banks. 'About that man Banks.'

'Yes?' said Roger.

'We've found him dead in his room, sir. The gas was full on, and the doors and windows sealed up. He killed himself, I should think. Will you come over?'

'Yes,' said Roger promptly. 'Don't touch anything.'

The only thing of interest at Banks' room, however, was the Michisons' address, with a note by it, saying: '*12 midnight*'. It was almost certain that this man had been at Michison's place, and attacked Sloan. He must have taken those telephone calls, too. Banks had rented a small furnished flatlet, and had been found stretched at full length on the floor, with a gas ring and a gas fire full on but not lighted. There was nothing at the flat to connect him with Riordon, and Roger returned to the Yard, very much on edge for news of Amy Groves. It was waiting for him: she had been killed while cycling from her Hampstead home to Broadcasting House, swerved, and been run over by a bus while avoiding a man who had stepped into the road: the man, who had hurried away, was not known.

'And he won't be, yet,' thought Roger grimly.

Some five minutes afterwards, while he was assuring himself that nothing could be more depressing and that Riordon was too much for him, the telephone rang again. Eddie Day, who was examining some forged treasury notes under a microscope, groaned exaggeratedly. Roger lifted the telephone to be told that Inspector Cartwright of the Dorchester Police, and Mr Lessing, were on their way upstairs.

'Good, thanks,' said Roger.

In exactly half an hour he had heard what the dwarf named Richardson had said, and heard precisely what had followed Riordon's appearance on the scene. Moreover he weighted the harmonica in his right hand, while Eddie Day, who had been affecting interest in nothing but his forged notes, peered at it and said: 'That's a nice-looking instrument, isn't it? Had it treated for prints, Inspector?'

'Yes, we've done that,' said Cartwright.

'Oh good,' said Eddie, taking the instrument. 'Yes, it's a nice little job. In my spare time – when I had some spare time, before this perishing crime wave began – I used to play a bit.' He put the thing to his lips and gave a trial blow, causing great discord. 'Not *bad*,' he admitted. 'I wouldn't mind that myself.'

Roger hardly heard him, but went on to say: 'So we're quite safe in plunging on the Newbury district. If I could only remember exactly what that ruddy map looked like we might get somewhere.' He paused, and rubbed his chin. 'The dwarf might pop up again, too, if Riordon missed him and he meant what he said. There's not much chance that he was putting something over you, Mark, is there?'

Mark shrugged. 'It isn't impossible, but – oh, stop that row!' he broke off, as Eddie Day brayed on the harmonica. At Eddie's reproachful look he added: 'Sorry, but if you'd heard that thing played in earnest, you wouldn't be so fond of it.'

'It's a very nice little instrument, this is,' insisted Eddie, 'but the C sharp's blocked up with something. If it wasn't for that I'd give you a tune you wouldn't forget.' As he spoke he took a penknife from his pocket, opened a very thin blade, and began to poke at the harmonica.

'Well, we can go to Woodhill,' Roger said. 'That won't do any harm. We can talk to Marion, and we'll be fairly near Newbury. Nearer than we are here, anyhow.'

'Good,' said Mark briefly.

Eddie Day, meanwhile, poked to good effect. He lost himself in that task, and finally hooked a small rolled ball of paper from the C sharp. He let it roll onto the desk, gave a triumphant blow up and down the scale, and then said: '*Now* listen to me!'

'Stop that!' said Roger, so sharply that Eddie did not get the harmonica to his lips but stared as Roger picked up the ball of paper. Mark and Cartwright watched him as intently while he unrolled the paper until it was flattened out, creased and dirty but quite unmistakably a map.

'The map!' exclaimed Mark.

'Is it the same one? *Is* it?' demanded Eddie Day.

A Place on the Map

ROGER'S HANDS shook as he looked down at the map. Mark and Eddie Day stared at him, and in the silence the rustling of the paper was clearly audible. Actually the silence did not last long, for Roger raised his head and said quietly: 'Yes, it's the same map.'

Mark sat down abruptly on the arm of a chair.

'You as sure as that, Handsome?' asked Eddie Day. 'You wouldn't like me to put it under the mike, would you, just to be sure?' He put a hand out for the map, and Roger let him take it, saying: 'All right, Eddie. You'll see a tiny asterisk in the top left hand corner – the mark I made. It's smudged, but it's unmistakable.'

'I'll soon check up on that,' Eddie said, and pushed the paper beneath the microscope. While he was adjusting the lenses Roger leaned across the desk and lifted the receiver, asking for the Drawing Office.

'Is Inspector Cross there?' he asked when someone answered, and after a pause went on: 'It's West here, old man . . . who's the best man you've got to make some quick tracings of a map . . . no, it needn't be an expert cartographer, I only want rough outlines.' He paused, and then went on: 'I'd rather have it done here . . . yes, half an hour will do fine. Many thanks. And what's the name of the man who knows all about maps . . . ah, I remember now, Palmerston. Yes, I have his number.'

He replaced the receiver as Eddie Day began: 'Why don't you have it—'

'Photographed,' said Roger for him. 'I'm going to, but this time I'm taking no chances at all. If you really want to do me a service,' he added, 'you can telephone a man named Palmerston – his number's in my book – and ask him if he'll come over right away. He's the owner of a firm of map-makers in Fleet Street,' he added briefly. 'Will you fix that for me?'

'You'd get blood out of a stone,' complained Eddie with a toothy smile. 'When you get on a case, Handsome, anyone would think there wasn't anything else worth worrying about in all England. All right, I'll do it you old twister.'

'One day I'll put a special word in for you with the Old Man,' Roger assured him.

'Well, that's very nice of you, very nice indeed,' said Eddie quite seriously. He was obsessed by the need for impressing Chatsworth, and was more scared of the AC than any other Inspector at the Yard. Roger did not smile, but led the other two men out of the office, walking towards the nearest stairs and mounting them rapidly while holding the map in his hand.

Neither Cartwright nor Mark spoke.

Roger opened an unmarked door on the second floor, entering a long, low-ceilinged room with a bench running along one side. A dozen men in shirtsleeves were working there, many of them taking plates out of large cameras at the bench: the room was a cross between a laboratory and a photographer's shop. At the far end, also in his shirtsleeves and wearing a bilious-looking yellow tie, was a rotund man with a pallid, flabby face, who looked up expressionlessly with his underlip drooping. ''Lo, Handsome,' he said.

'Can you do a really high-speed job for me?'

'Never known anything I can't do in this room,' declared the rotund man in a ridiculously low voice. 'What is it?' He took the map which Roger held out, pulled at his underlip, and nodded gently. 'Sure,' he said, and then raised his voice so that it boomed above every other sound in the room. *'Teddy! Teddy!'*

A vague-looking man came ambling from the long bench.

'Be as quick as you can with that,' said the Yard's photographic expert, Inspector Lloyd Williams. 'I want three prints in ten minutes. Ten minutes be all right for you, Handsome?'

'Fine,' said Roger. 'And another twenty or thirty prints soon. Can you fix it?'

'Never known anything I can't do in this room,' repeated Williams, soft-voiced again. 'I've some other prints for you. *Charley!*' His voice boomed out again. 'Those prints for the Inspector, at the double now.' Williams pulled at his underlip until he revealed all his front lower teeth, and then added softly: 'I never have a minute to breathe, never a minute. Photographs! I'm getting tired of the very word, and if anyone says "camera" to me I'll throw one at him. Introduce me, Handsome, can't you? Not to Mr Lessing, of course, we're old friends. Still putting up with our Handsome, Mr Lessing?' Williams did not smile, but spoke while pulling at his lips; his eyes were quite expressionless, a weak, watery grey.

'Chief Inspector Cartwright, of the Dorchester police,' said Roger. 'Cartwright, this is the man who always gets things done when they're wanted, and not half an hour later.'

'I'm going back to Dorchester to fix things up there,' said Cartwright warmly. 'This is really first class, Inspector.'

From a cubicle on one side of the room came a tall, weary-looking man carrying several large prints. He put them down without a word, and turned away. Williams began to run through the photographs which had typewritten captions at the bottom.

Three were of Sergeant Sloan's battered head, another of the room where he had been lying. There were photographs of Amy Groves, Banks, and Allen, of Lionel Michison, Commander Morris, and Sir William Bennett.

'All right?' asked Williams.

'Can I take one of each?' asked Roger.

'What do you think they're there for?' demanded Williams.

'Teddy, what the blazes is delaying you? Teddy!'

The first man came up, carrying three dripping prints from the darkroom. The map was reproduced in even greater clarity than the original printed drawing. Teddy apologised because they would need drying, but asked whether they were all right: he had the original with him.

Five minutes later, when the trio left the Photographic Department with everything they required, Cartwright said in some astonishment: 'That's one of the most amazing things I've ever seen. Is it always like that?'

'Pretty nearly,' said Roger. 'Williams is right on top of his job.'

So, it proved, were others; for a pale young man came from the Drawing Department with the necessary paper and impedimenta for making tracings of the map.

Palmerston arrived soon afterwards. He was a small, neatly-dressed man who gave an impression of shyness. He heard exactly what Roger wanted of him, said that he would do his best, and, with large-scale Ordnance maps of the Newbury district spread out on Roger's desk, began his task. Roger decided that there was no need to sit and watch him, and ran through many reports that had come in. Eddie Day made some tea and dispensed it genially, while Mark took the opportunity of telephoning Marion at Woodhill 35.

Marion answered the telephone herself.

She had nothing to report except the presence of several men in the vicinity whom the landlord of the inn where she was staying declared to be 'busies' from Newbury. Mark assured her that it was not unexpected, and told her that he hoped to be there within three hours. He was smiling when he rang off.

It was just after four o'clock when Palmerston coughed to attract attention.

Four men, including Eddie Day, looked up and started to move at the same time.

'Any luck?' Roger asked eagerly.

'I think I can identify the district,' said Palmerston primly. 'If I am right, then this rough map was traced over one half the scale of those I am using. I should say that the places indicated are Highclere' – he pointed to one of the dots – 'Whitway,

Kingsclere, Newtown, and, right down here due south of Newbury, Lichfield. Of course, there's no absolute certainty, but the distance between the places and their actual location are precisely the same, assuming that the map from which it was traced was half-scale to these.'

'Good man,' said Roger slowly. 'So our place should be somewhere south or south-east of Newbury. Where is Woodhill, a little village not far away?'

'I think—' began Palmerston, turning to the map, 'that it's – yes, here it is. Between Reading and Aldermaston, nearer Aldermaston, and about ten miles from Newbury. Is that all right?'

'You couldn't have done better,' Roger assured him.

When the tracings were finished and more prints had come from the soft-voiced Williams, the names of the villages were hurriedly written in. That was done while Roger was interviewing Chatsworth, who followed the story keenly and looked more hopeful than he had for some time. Roger thought, as he looked at the AC, that Chatsworth was probably having an extremely difficult time with the Home Office, and perhaps with the Cabinet. The importance of a speedy solution had never been more apparent.

Only one thing seriously worried Roger, and he tried not to dwell too much upon it.

Deliberately, and with great cunning, Riordon had set out to draw red herrings across his path. The very existence of the map, as well as the play Riordon had made with it, might prove another of even greater proportions: if so, if they were being led into a trap, the possibilities were disturbing to say the least. He did not voice his suspicions to Chatsworth, but at the back of his mind thought that Chatsworth probably considered them.

'Well, good luck,' said the AC as Roger finished. 'You'll get all the support you need from the people at Newbury, of course, and I take it you've telephoned them to look around.'

'Of course, sir,' said Roger.

'Good, that's good. Don't let them do too much on their own, mind you, I don't want Riordon let loose amongst a lot of country cops.' Chatsworth grinned unexpectedly. 'That's a bit hard on the Berkshire and Hampshire people isn't it. Good chaps, I believe. Still, you know what I mean. How many men are you taking from here?'

'Three or four will be enough, I think,' said Roger.

'All right. Er – but you might need stronger forces. Going to call in the Army if you think it's necessary? You'd better, whether you want to or not. I'll get in touch with them and see that you don't have any difficulty. Er – you do understand the full importance of this, don't you, West?'

'I don't think I underrate it,' Roger said.

'We must get those people Riordon's taken out of his hands alive,' said Chatsworth sharply. 'Some of them don't count all that much, but even they are human beings and it's our job to save 'em whatever kind of life they'll have afterwards. But those nine or ten key-men – the nation needs 'em, West. *Needs* 'em. Well – Aldermaston,' he added. 'Nasty possibilities there.'

'You mean, the atomic research station.'

'Of course I do.'

'I can't believe Riordon would have his headquarters there if he was planning trouble in the vicinity,' Roger said. 'But I'll alert the security forces there.'

Half an hour later two large cars left Scotland Yard. There were four men in each, and each man carried an automatic. There were supplies of tear gas and everything that Roger imagined might be needed if it came to a straightforward fight with Riordon's unknown minions. He did not think that he was overdramatising the situation, and was filled with an intense anxiety to see the end of it that day.

Yet all the time the fear that Riordon had prepared an enormous booby trap worried him. To get to the nearest village, Newtown, it was necessary to go through Reading and to pass within a mile of Woodhill. It was still very warm, although white puffs of cloud appeared in the sky, and there were cirrus clouds arrayed in superb symmetry high above their heads. They went past wooded land and meadows, over tiny streams, once they were off the main road and heading for Woodhill itself. It was a village right off the beaten track, and halfway up a wooded hill which they would see from the main road. The hill's serried masses of trees, mostly beech and oak but with dark-hued copper beech breaking the restfulness of the deep green, drew gradually nearer as they went up the steep road. It was in bad repair.

Mark was smoking a cigarette, and Roger imagined something of the tension in his friend's mind.

Then they turned a corner, and Roger, at the wheel, had the first glimpse of Woodhill. He saw thatched cottages cheek-by-jowl with small modern houses built by an architect who knew how to merge the new with the old. On either side of the road were attractive modern houses standing in gardens of half an acre or more. At the foot of the hill, which they could see well from the road, a stream meandered: and along the road walked two old men in waders, carrying fishing rods and baskets.

Then they saw the inn, a low-roofed, stone-built place, with trim cypresses on either side, and a newly painted sign: *The Trout and the Fly*. Roger saw that, but Mark had eyes only for Marion Byrne who was standing on the cobbled yard outside. When she saw him she hurried forward, smiling and tense. Mark left the car before it had really stopped: and then, quite absurdly, the couple shook hands.

Roger heard Marion say: 'Mark, it's good to see you! You *are* all right?' She looked into his eyes while his devoured her, and then added quickly: 'Is that Roger West?'

'It is,' said Roger, approaching more leisurely. 'This is a pleasant place to spend a holiday, anyhow.'

'Holiday!' exclaimed Marion with a grimace. She was very good to look at with the sun shining on her fair hair and her blue eyes very bright. She wore a fresh-looking green frock, and sandals.

'Well, hasn't it been?' he said.

He felt a sense of anticlimax, and for the first time wondered whether it would have been wiser had he gone straight on to Newbury. But he wanted to make sure that she could tell him nothing else, and that within already known limits she could confirm what Richardson the dwarf had told them. Until they saw the Newbury police, moreover, there was little he could do.

'No,' said Marion. 'But as Mark advised me to stay here I thought I'd better. How long are you going to stay?' she asked Roger. 'I should think you've sent luggage enough for a month.'

Roger stared at her. 'What luggage?'

'Well, if it isn't luggage, what is it?' demanded Marion. 'A cabin trunk came for you this morning, marked "To await arrival".'

'I sent no trunk,' said Roger.

'Well, it's here,' said Marion.

She looked puzzled, while Mark and Roger exchanged glances and Cartwright appeared very thoughtful. 'It's standing in the hall. It wasn't taken upstairs in case you wanted to move it again.'

They went in a bunch towards the low doorway of the inn, and entered quickly. It was dark and shadowy inside, but there was charm about it not unlike that of the cottage. By the foot of the stairs was a large trunk covered with green canvas and with leather at the corners; it had passed its first youth. Painted on it were the initials 'R.W.', and the label read as Marion had said.

'Aren't you going to open it?' Marion demanded.

Roger said slowly: 'Yes. But I don't know that I'm keen about what we're going to find.'

Then he went down on one knee, taking out a key case as he did so. The thing that disturbed him most was that it *was* his trunk. There was no doubt about it, and it should have been in the loft of the Bell Street house.

Contents of a Trunk

ROGER DID NOT KNOW why he wished that Marion was not standing near him, looking so eagerly at the box. Several thoughts flashed through his mind but he had actually put the key in the lock when he had a mental vision of a radiogram at the Michisons' flat, the one which had exploded without warning. The chance that this was another such infernal machine loomed large in his mind's eye. He took the key out and said quietly: 'On second thoughts we'll open it outside. And as there's just a chance that there's a catch in it I'll do it myself.'

'What kind of a catch?' demanded Cartwright.

Roger said: 'Riordon dabbles in pyrotechnics.' He sounded vague as he motioned to two of his men to lift the trunk, telling them to handle it carefully. They stepped outside, and placed it gently on the cobbles. Then, at Roger's instructions, they moved back. Several villagers, intrigued by what was happening, joined the circle.

'You'd be wiser to move, too,' Roger said to Mark.

'I never was a Solomon,' murmured Mark. 'Get it over.'

'Right! Here goes,' said Roger briskly.

He inserted the key again, and turned it; the lock moved easily. He took one corner of the lid, and Mark took the other. They were conscious of Marion, Cartwright, and the Yard men craning their necks to get a better view of the contents when the lid was pushed back, as they lifted it gently. At first there was nothing at all, and they could see only the dark void inside;

the trunk was not filled to the top.

Still gently, still fearful of a trap and even expecting an explosion, Roger eased the lid right back and peered inside: Mark did the same, and it was Mark who uttered the first exclamation. It sprang from his lips in a mingling of shock and surprise.

'My God!' he exclaimed, and jumped up. Marion, moving forward, said: 'What is—'

'Don't go any nearer!' Mark ordered sharply. He had lost his colour, and when his hand touched her wrist it was very cold. Roger continued to look inside the case, at the naked, terribly mutilated body of a little creature whose face was untouched.

It was Richardson the dwarf.

The only thing to be done Roger thought as he straightened up, was to find who had delivered the trunk and trace them. He felt sickened by the sight of that dreadfully treated body: it looked as if the instrument used to kill Parker and injure Sloan had been used on the dwarf, except his head. His face, no longer red, was set in lines which suggested that he had been conscious while most of the injuries had been inflicted.

'We'll have it taken into Newbury,' he said half to himself, 'and get it photographed there.' In a loud voice: 'Strap it on the luggage carrier of one of the cars, will you?' As he spoke he pulled the lid down and relocked the box, then went straight into *The Trout and the Fly* and asked a man in a green baize apron and shirtsleeves for the telephone. He called the Newbury police. When they were on the line he called the man who stood near his elbow.

'What time did the box arrive?'

'Be about ten this morning, sir.'

'*Ten?*'

'That's it – no, wait a minute! That was time the carrier came. It wasn't delivered by him, came by the bus. Heavy case it was for the bus, sir. About two o'clock, that would be.'

'Whose bus was it?'

'Why, the local from Newbury, to be sure.'

'Thanks,' said Roger. By then the Superintendent at Newbury was on the line. He asked for the local bus driver to be interrogated, and efforts made to trace the way the trunk had been delivered to it, and then went on to ask: 'Have you any news for me?'

In a deep voice, the Newbury man said: 'I don't know that I have, Handsome. I've had a list prepared of all the possible houses, and except for one they're either occupied by their owners, or tenants. The other one is derelict – it was burned down years ago. It's hardly worth it, I'd say, to bother to repair it. It's in a pretty bad state.'

Slowly, Roger said: 'And there's nowhere else at all?'

'I know every man and woman in the district who live in houses that size,' said the Superintendent. 'I can vouch for each one. I'll guarantee that there's no one in that district you've detailed who would have anything to do with the Riordon business. Mind you, I'm having inquiries made for comings and goings, but I'm not very hopeful.'

Half-desperately, Roger said: 'What about hotels or private guest houses?'

'Since I first had a description of Riordon I've had a lookout kept for him,' replied the Superintendent. 'He hasn't been seen in the vicinity, and if the description I've had is accurate he isn't a man who would be easily mistaken.'

'Oh, he'd be recognised,' Roger said gloomily. 'Will you mind trying a bit more? I'll be in your office within an hour. I've a job for your photographers, too. By the way, does Woodhill come under your area, or Reading's?'

'Mine.'

'Then you'll want to know more about that cabin trunk I've been making inquiries about,' said Roger, and passed on the news.

Obviously it was something of a shock, and the Superintendent promised very prompt action. Roger was reluctant to hang up the receiver, for some reason which he could not explain, but he was about to do so after saying 'goodbye' when he thought he heard the Superintendent shout. He put the receiver to his ear again.

'West, are you still there?'

'Yes, what is it?'

'I thought you'd gone,' said the Superintendent. 'Just a moment, there's a report about the bus driver.'

'That's quick work!'

'It's not part of our inquiry,' said the Newbury man. 'We don't deal in thought reading yet. Ah, here's the chap.' Roger heard him speak to someone else in the office. '*What!* You're sure?' Another voice sounded, too far away for Roger to hear what was said, and the wait seemed a very long one. Then the Superintendent spoke again; his voice had lost something of its depth because of excitement. 'West, are you there? . . . That bus driver. The bus didn't get into Newbury when it should, and has been found ditched not far from Woodhill. Over the other side of the hill. The driver's dead. He was smashed up when the bus crashed, as far as I can tell you.'

Roger said very slowly: 'So Riordon's *very* anxious to prevent me from knowing where that trunk was put on the bus?'

'You think ' began the Superintendent.

'Is it reasonable to call it an accident?' demanded Roger. 'Much more likely he was killed to prevent him from talking. It isn't likely that he could give anything away unless he took the trunk from someone he knew. That would surely be someone in this region.'

The Superintendent said: 'Probably. I don't like the way this is working out. What will you do?'

'I think I'll go and see that bus,' said Roger. 'Will the local people know the route it took?'

He was assured that they would, and then rang off.

He stepped away from the telephone, almost knocking against the little man in the green baize apron, who accompanied him as far as the door, walking almost on his heels and irritating him, although he forebore comment. The man told him in aggrieved tones that he was the host of the inn, and then: 'What's happened to the bus driver?' he demanded. 'He had some parcels to deliver for me, haven't they turned up?'

'They will,' said Roger, 'and—'

He stopped abruptly, and stiffened.

Marion and Mark, just outside the front door, were nearer him than Cartwright or the Yard men, and consequently they were just able to hear the sound which had so great an effect on him. They stared towards the house and the open door, while the little man looked round as if startled.

Very faintly but clearly came the strains of the *Warsaw Concerto*. It sounded as if it came from the same instrument as Richardson had used. It drew nearer, although it did not get very close to them, and it continued through the tense quiet to its end, then it stopped as abruptly as it had begun.

'The Trout and the Fly'

'DID YOU HEAR *that*?' demanded the little man, standing with his mouth agape and his hands on his hips. 'That toon?'

With an effort Roger said: 'I heard it.'

'Does it make sense?' Mark put the question slowly and looked paler even than when he had peered into the trunk. 'I'm sure that Richardson's in there. Yet—'

'It wasn't Richardson, and it wasn't his mouth organ,' said Roger, trying to be matter-of-fact. 'It might have been another dwarf and another instrument.' He looked at the gaping landlord and said abruptly: 'How many guests are staying here?'

'Six or seven,' the man said. 'What are you getting at? What's the matter with you?'

'Landlord, this place is under police jurisdiction until further notice,' Roger said. He took out his warrant card, half-expecting an outburst of indignant protest, but none was forthcoming, the little man simply looked dazed. Roger went on briskly: 'I'll need to search the rooms right away.'

'Search my pub?' the man gasped.

'Here and now,' said Roger, looking at the group of Yard men and motioning them towards the door.

They moved past Marion and Mark, and they were about to pass Roger and enter the hall when someone else spoke from inside the inn. Roger recognised the voice on the instant and with the first syllable. He swung round, stopping his men with a gesture, for it was Riordon's voice.

Riordon said from inside *The Trout and the Fly:* 'Searching won't do you any good, West. You are not going to have the chance, anyhow. You have walked right into disaster. I knew you would, but you were a long time coming.'

Marion exclaimed: 'Who—'

Mark put a hand at her mouth.

'There was a time when I did not think you would stop me,' Riordon went on. 'I thought this place was nicely hidden, but when that misshapen beast' – venom sounded in his voice – 'walked out on me, I knew that would be the end. Well, it *might*. It will make no difference to me, you will never stop me although I cannot go ahead with this particular scheme. That is a great pity.'

Roger said slowly: 'It's going to make all the difference in the world to you.'

'Oh no, it isn't,' said Riordon. 'You are cornered, don't you understand? You are covered from all directions. If you come into the place you will be stopped. If you try to leave by car you will be stopped. There are thirty-nine houses and cottages in Woodhill, and twenty-one of them are mine. I actually had them built. Understand me – this is *my* village. All the people do not know it, but it's mine all right, and if there should be anyone who wants trouble, he can start interfering now. Richardson did not know about this, you see, I kept something from him. Never trust any man all the way, West.'

Roger said with an effort: 'What would you like for an obituary?'

'That is not funny!' snapped Riordon. 'That is not a bit funny. If you make more bad jokes you will suffer more than I intend at the moment. Then there is Lessing.' The way he sneered the name made Mark flinch. The deep voice seemed to come from somewhere hollow as if the man was talking from inside a cave. Or, more likely, thought Roger, through a microphone. 'Then there is Lessing,' Riordon went on. 'I told him that I would make him understand what pain was really like. And I will.'

'There's an old story about the long arm of the law, too,' said

Roger. 'So you think you'll get away with this?'

'I know I will,' said Riordon. He seemed to have no doubt at all, and there was something unnerving in his confidence. 'Perhaps I will not be able to take all the guests away' – something that might have been a ghostly laugh followed the words – 'but I will make sure they are not any good to you or your damned country. Do you know that I have got German and Irish blood in my veins? That is a good mixture when it comes to hating the English. And I hate them so much I want to destroy their atomic power – all the industrial know-how from the atom. That is why I wanted the men I have got, the scientists and physicists and civil servants. They are key-men, but if you have to rely on halfwits like them for your programme you will not get very far. The United States and the Russians would gladly buy what I can offer.'

'Do you know the penalty for treason?'

'I know about everything,' boasted Riordon. 'Well, what are you going to do? How many of you are here?' He began to count. 'One, two, three . . . seven, eight, nine altogether, including Maid Marion.' He sneered again. 'You're outnumbered three to one. Does that give you any of your bright ideas?'

Roger said: 'I'm full of them.'

'All right, then, demonstrate,' sneered Riordon.

Very deliberately, Roger smiled.

He did not feel like smiling for he was completely at a loss. He was wholly convinced that Riordon was telling the truth, and that the police were outnumbered three to one; the possibility was too great to be ignored. He realised that Riordon was in an upstairs room and that the slight distortion of his voice came from a microphone: probably the *Concerto* had come from that, played very faintly to attract their attention. Riordon had far too many tricks up his sleeve.

That kind of reflection was a waste of time.

What was his best course of action? Was he to give orders to the men, whom he knew would obey without question, to rush the inn? If he did the danger of having them wiped out was considerable. But even beyond that immediate problem was something greater. *Was* the whole of this village owned by the man? Were the missing scientists and the whole party of officials actually in Woodhill? Were the missing women here? Some forty people, he thought, living here under duress; was it possible?

Sickeningly, he admitted that it was. One person to each house would cover it, and *The Trout and the Fly* probably had room for ten. He thought of the casualness with which he had first considered the inn, and then wondered again about Marion. Was she quite innocent of all complicity?

'That doesn't matter,' he told himself. 'It doesn't matter. All that matters is to stop Riordon.' He thought of the Newbury police who were waiting for him and of the Home Guards and military, doubtless ready to lend a hand if one were needed. It had never been more necessary, but he could think of no way of getting a message to them.

He might try to run the gauntlet of Riordon's men. Even if they were as numerous as the man claimed there was a chance of getting away in one of the cars. One door was standing open, and he could see the controls: the seat looked very inviting. Two men were standing behind it, and the trunk containing Richardson's body was already on the carrier.

'Go on, take your time,' sneered Riordon.

'We can't get outside help quickly,' thought Roger. 'We simply can't get it. We've got to handle this ourselves.' Helplessly he wondered which of the houses were under Riordon's direct control, and he thought of the weapons which had been brought down. Automatics, a single tommy gun which was inside one of the cars, and not immediately available, and tear gas. He had a supply in his pocket, but little else that would do any good. The long inn, which seemed to stretch for a long way on either side of the front door, gave no cover at all from the three or four houses immediately opposite: only the trim cypresses could give even a pretence of cover.

'Where's the white flag?' demanded Riordon.

After a long pause Mark broke his long silence. 'Don't you know?' he demanded.

He was holding Marion's arm. The girl was very pale, although her eyes were brilliant; too brilliant, thought Roger. Her lips were set, and obviously she was very much afraid. For that matter the tension amongst the other men was unmistakable: Cartwright was affected as well as all the Yard men. Small wonder in that, thought Roger, and then wondered why Riordon was waiting so long.

Was it just to increase the suspense?

'Or isn't he ready for us yet?' Roger wondered, the thought flashing across his mind. 'He's probably waiting to get himself and his men into position.'

'Not a bad idea,' said Mark.

He spoke in a low-pitched voice, surprising Roger, who had not realised that he had uttered the words aloud. He saw the pressure of Mark's hand increase on Marion's arm, and yet was not really surprised when Mark suddenly released her and made a dive for the nearest car.

It was no more than five yards away from him. The open door was almost in his reach when there was a single bark of a shot from somewhere inside *The Trout and the Fly*. Mark looked as if he missed his footing. He went down heavily, half-rose, gasped, and fell back again. Roger did not know where he had been hit, but felt a sickening sense of futility. Marion half-turned.

'Stay there,' said Riordon harshly. 'No one will move towards Lessing, or they will get the same as he did.'

'We must help him,' Marion exclaimed urgently.

'Wait a moment,' said Roger, staring towards Mark. 'It's his leg, I think.' He could hardly hear his own voice, but could see that there was blood making Mark's flannel trousers dark: the wound was halfway up his thigh.

He thought: 'It's not fatal, it shouldn't have put him right out like that.'

A moment later he realised that it had not. He saw Mark

move his head an inch from the ground, then saw the pressure he was putting on his hands. He was going forward, trying to crawl towards the car without being seen. Roger experienced a fierce temptation to join him, but repressed it. It would be far better if he did something to distract Riordon's attention; that was far more important.

He spoke quietly but loudly enough to everyone to hear.

'Stay there, all of you. Keep by the wall, Marion.'

'Where are you—' Marion began to ask, but stopped when she saw him step towards the open door. As he went the little innkeeper stepped in front of him and looked up at him with a leer.

'No you don't, mister.'

'Don't I?' asked Roger.

He shot out a hand and pushed the little man aside, obviously taking the fellow by surprise for his victim went sprawling over a coconut mat outside the doorway. Ignoring him, Roger stepped into the shadowy hall.

His mind was working furiously. He saw the chance which might be taken. If Mark could get off in the car he would telephone for help from the nearest callbox. If there was one three miles away it would be ten minutes or a little more before the Newbury Police had the alarm. In their state of preparedness they would be ready to move, so they could arrive within the hour. There was even a chance that there was a military camp which could be warned to send men even more quickly.

The one essential was to have the village surrounded. There was no alteration in one inevitable fact: the initial work had to be done by the party in the village. Not the final round-up, thought Roger, but the delaying operations to prevent Riordon and his men getting away. It was possible; it had to be made possible.

'If the men are in various houses he can't do anything to them all at once,' he thought.

These ideas flashed through his mind in the brief moment as he stepped swiftly to the right of the main door, going towards a low-ceilinged dining room: he could see the tables set for dinner, and the sun, coming through a low window, was shining on glasses and cutlery. As he reached the door of the dining room, the wall of the inn was between him and the road, and there was no direct approach to the spot from the inn itself.

'That helps,' he said.

He put his hand to his pocket and drew out a small, wooden case. He opened it quickly, revealing half a dozen small glass tubes filled with golden crystals: they looked like the crystals of Demerara sugar. He pulled one of the tubes out and tossed it towards the stairs, able to aim for it without doing more than show his hand.

He hoped that what wind there was would blow from the rear of the inn.

He heard the tinkle of breaking glass, and, after a few seconds, caught the first faint smell of the gas; his eyes began to irritate a little and to fill with tears. He stepped farther into the dining room, far less concerned with what was happening to him than with what was being done outside. One thing was remarkable; since he had moved Riordon had not spoken and nothing had been done.

There was nothing normal about it, thought Roger; it was fantastic, had been eerie from the very beginning. The material explanations must exist, but that did not make it easier to understand just then.

He disliked the quiet; there was something ominous in it, an unspoken menace which would surely be translated into action before long. Riordon's silence began to get on his nerves: it seemed to tell him mockingly that he had failed in his main objective of distracting attention from Mark.

Then he heard the whirr of a self-starter, and fast upon it came the snorting note of an engine starting.

Although his heart leapt with the hope that Mark was making a getaway, and although the quiet was broken by the noise of the engine, at the back of his mind there was a sense of fear because of the strange immobility of Riordon and his men;

he was tempted to leave the temporary cover he had found, for more reasons than one. The tear gas was getting stronger, and tears were beginning to trickle down his cheeks. He thought of the possibility that he would suffer more than Riordon for the gas attack. He had a premonition that the end was very near for him. Riordon's self-confidence was not ordinary; there must be some unsuspected reason for it.

He was waiting there when he heard Marion cry out.

Then he heard footsteps and guessed that she was running across the cobbled yard. A moment later the rending crash of a car in collision drowned all other sounds. It seemed to last for a long time but gradually grew fainter; Marion's footsteps grew audible again.

There was something else; there were heavy footsteps on the stairs, and the sound of a man coughing.

Pep Morgan Reappears

THE FOOTSTEPS told their story.

In spite of the way his eyes were watering and the irritation at his nose and throat, Roger felt a fierce exhilaration: those footsteps on the stairs were of a man who limped: one heavy, one light – the kind of footsteps that Riordon would make when hurrying. And there was a harshness in the coughing which seemed to come from Riordon.

Had the tear gas affected him?

Roger put his hand to his pocket and drew farther back into the dining room. He was within easy range of the houses on the other side of the road, but for the moment ignored that. He drew out an automatic, while the heavy footsteps drew nearer. Then he thought of the back entrance and the chance that Riordon would choose that way of escape.

Was Riordon smoked out and running away?

Roger stepped into the passage swiftly, and as he did so he saw Riordon at the foot of the stairs. The man's face was covered with tears, and his mouth was wide open as he took in great gulps of gas-laden air. He looked ogrish and unnatural, for his face was red instead of pale; and his eyes were closed.

The simple things work, thought Roger.

Blindly, Riordon turned at the foot of the stairs and went towards a closed door. Roger kept his lips compressed, tried to hold his breath, and then fired towards the man's legs. At first the shots took no effect. Riordon groped for the handle of the door, found it, and pulled it open. Roger fired again, and from the back of the inn came a soft wind, dispersing much of the gas and giving Roger a chance to gulp in the clear air. He moved forward, but before he reached the stairs Riordon stumbled and pitched forward on his face.

'Got him!' exclaimed Roger aloud. 'We've got him!'

He began to cough, but could not stop himself from going farther forward. He was wary of Riordon whom he could see only vaguely through a film of tears. There was no indication of anything amiss outside, although he expected sounds of fighting very soon. He thought of Marion and Mark and the other man there, wondered whether they were covered by Riordon's men. And why Riordon had suddenly stopped talking? Why had so much been allowed to happen?

He was within a yard of the man when Riordon moved.

Until then the man had been lying face downwards, with his arms above his head. His hands, as far as Roger could see, were empty. The next moment he turned, a monstrous figure seen through the tears, and rose to his knees in a swift, twisting movement. He put his right hand to his pocket.

Roger fired at him; but at his chest. As he did so he remembered what had happened to Mark's hand after punching at Riordon, and thought of the steel waistcoat. The bullet would be wasted. Certainly it had no effect. The man took something from his pocket. Roger could not see what it was, but before he could fire again Riordon flung it. Something struck Roger on the side of his head, making him stagger back. His eyes closed and he could see nothing, but he heard a grunt as if Riordon were making a supreme effort.

Then the man closed with him.

Had he been able to see the way Riordon flung himself upwards from his knees he would have marvelled at it, for it seemed impossible to do. As it was he felt the weight of the man's body bearing him down. He thought fleetingly that Riordon had foxed him right to the end, for the man could not have been hit. Then he felt the man's great fingers closing about his throat.

There was a drumming noise in his ears, but other sounds penetrated from outside. He thought he heard the staccato bark of a machine gun or a tommy gun, but could not be sure. Then awareness of anything but his own immediate plight faded. Riordon's harsh breathing was close to his ears and he could feel hot breath on his face. He remembered the twisted features, knew that Riordon was fighting against the effect of the tear gas, just as much as he. But it did not seem to rob the man of any strength; the grip of his fingers increased, blackness surged over Roger, and he felt weak and helpless. He tried to struggle and to bring his knees up into the pit of his adversary's stomach, but failed. He felt the dreadful pressure increasing remorselessly, his head was swimming, his thoughts were incoherent. Then the grip relaxed without warning.

He could not understand it, and did not hear the gasp as Riordon let him go. Nor did he see the little, shiny-faced man who stood behind Riordon and struck at his head with the butt end of a revolver. He fell to the floor, aware of nothing, certainly not realising that Riordon was also on the floor again, not gasping but with his features twisting and his body twitching.

Roger felt someone pull at his legs, but could not try to prevent himself being dragged away. His head went over soft carpet, then over something cold and shiny, then bumped against what seemed like stone. After a few seconds of that the man stopped pulling him.

He was aware of clearer air; the stifling effect of the tear gas was gone, although he still felt ill and was seized with a paroxysm of coughing which shook his whole frame. After the bout he was limp and exhausted but grew aware of light in front of his eyes. He knew that he was alive, and, for the first time since Riordon had tried to strangle him, his thoughts were coherent. He heard more sounds, that of heavy breathing and of something heavy being dragged from the inn: and he heard two words in a familiar voice.

'Not bad.' It was Pep Morgan, the inquiry agent who had

already helped in the investigations. 'Not bad.'

'Pep!' croaked Roger.

'Don't you start talking yet,' said Morgan. 'You're in no shape for talking, Handsome.' The words sounded as if they were spoken a long way off. 'Nor is *this* customer. We've got him, we've got him. You did wonders, absolute wonders.' There was a pause, and then in a sharper voice: 'Are *you* all right, sir?'

Someone else had loomed up, a vague figure which Roger could not see clearly, and again he identified a man by his voice.

'Yes, Morgan, don't worry about me. How's West?' A pause, and then: 'So we smoked Riordon out, did we. *Very* nice indeed. But I don't think West will be very pleased with us, do you? He'll feel that we put one over him.'

Roger thought incredulously: 'That's Chatsworth!'

Roger soon learned that Morgan and Chatsworth with a strong force of police were near at hand, and that soon the village was filled with khaki-clad figures. He knew, too, that Riordon remained unconscious and there was a gaping wound in his head where Pep Morgan had hit him. He had no idea how Pep had managed to get into the inn, nor how Chatsworth had appeared on the scene. The only consideration of importance was Riordon's complete rout; it did not matter how it had happened.

Marion was all right: Mark, Pep told him as he hurried through the little yard at the back of the inn, had been knocked about a bit when the car had crashed. Someone had fired at it from a window and struck the steering wheel. Cartwright and the other Yard men had not been hurt, although they had been kept immobile by a tommy gun poking from a window opposite. Then, when Cartwright and two others had taken a chance, the shooting had prevented them: they had taken cover behind the remaining car.

Other thoughts crowded Roger's mind. Did Chatsworth

know that Riordon had owned the village, had he any knowledge of the occupants of the various houses? It was time he moved and took more interest in what was happening.

He was sitting on a wooden bench at the back of *The Trout and the Fly,* his eyes much better, his breathing steadier, and his limbs more biddable. Beyond him was a peaceful scene, of apple and pear trees, a well-dug vegetable patch, and, beyond that, a hen coop outside which a dozen fowls were pecking at the grass of their enclosure. Very peaceful, thought Roger; too peaceful, and holding a touch of fantasy like the rest of the case. Riordon was on the ground, still unconscious. Someone had tried to bathe his head but the matted hair was bare to the wind, and the bleeding continued. He could see the man's chest heaving as he tried to breathe. Near him was a heavy piece of wood, with several spikes sticking from it. There were brownish red stains on it, and he realised it was a particularly nasty truncheon; the wounds in Parker's head, and Sloan's, had probably been caused by it.

'Why leave him like this?' Roger thought. 'What are they playing at?'

Then, from a window, he heard Chatsworth's voice again. 'West, don't raise your voice. Can you hear me?'

Roger turned, startled, and saw Chatsworth's face half-hidden by net curtains at a window which was open a few inches at the bottom. Roger gulped, and nodded.

'You're well covered,' Chatsworth said. 'He won't get away. But I want to pretend that he has a chance. If he thinks that he's alone with you he might talk. Try to make him. Understand?'

Roger whispered: 'What do you want to know?'

'We've found the kidnapped women, but not the men we're after,' said Chatsworth briefly. 'Don't know where they are, either. Thought they were all here, but he's managed to get them away. Sure you understand?'

Very slowly, Roger said: 'Yes, I get you.'

So it was not over, and it had not been as easy as it appeared; Riordon had managed to outwit them again. Helpless and surrounded, Riordon still exerted that strange influence, still managed to hold a trump card. The men, who were absolutely vital, were still missing.

He felt very weary as he looked away when Chatsworth disappeared from the window.

A long time seemed to pass before Riordon stirred again.

Roger saw the man's eyes flicker; they opened for a moment, and closed again. His body moved convulsively. There was blood on his trousers just above one knee; from the bullet wound which brought him down, thought Roger.

That did not matter: all that mattered was finding the men.

Then Riordon opened his eyes and did not close them again. He was looking at Roger, and continued to stare, the basilisk gaze not dimmed by the swollen, red-rimmed eyes but looking more evil because of them.

Riordon said: 'So *you're* still here.'

Roger said nothing.

'Where are the others?' demanded Riordon. His voice was thick but had little strength. 'Where are the others? The unspeakable swine deserted me. They promised to see me through, but they deserted. *And* they put me in this plight, too. Men I have worked with for years, curse them. For years! If I could reach them—'

He stopped, and Roger said as if very wearily: 'Shut up.'

'Where are the others?' demanded Riordon. '*Your* idiots – where are they?'

'Chasing off somewhere,' said Roger. 'After your friends.'

'And left you alone with *me?*'

'I'm no more important than you are,' said Roger. At least his mind was working well, and he saw a way of getting this man to talk more freely. 'We're the has-beens in this case. But you're cleverer than I thought.'

'You're telling me!' sneered Riordon.

Roger said: 'I don't know how you managed it. I thought we'd get all of you, but there's only you and a few of your roughnecks. At least we got the women,' he added very slowly.

'*They* won't suffer any more.'

Softly, Riordon said: 'What about the men? Your precious geniuses.'

Roger shrugged, but said nothing.

'So they have been taken away,' said Riordon, his voice growing stronger. 'They have got them away, have they?' There was a long pause, and Roger expected a vituperative outburst against the unknowns who had escaped with the hostages and left Riordon to his fate.

There was no such outburst.

A queer expression, hardly a smile and yet obviously intended for one, crossed Riordon's face. The intensity of his gaze increased. He looked nowhere else but at Roger, and after a long pause he said softly: 'Now *that* is what I call *clever*. They persuaded you and your police halfwits to concentrate on me, and escaped away with the prize which really matters. That is clever, West. I did not think they'd have the sense to do it. It is worth dying for,' he added, and the words struck a chill through Roger. 'And now I know what your hope is,' went on Riordon more harshly. 'You think I will talk. You are not good enough at this game, you want to retire and keep chickens.' He laughed, explosively. 'I thought I was the leader, I thought that they were helpless without me, but they are clever, they have foxed me but they have foxed you, too. And you thought I would betray them! You thought I would tell you where to find them. You thought I would care what happened to me! You damned fool! I am a bigger man than that, West. All I am interested in is defeating you and your big-headed Government. If I can do anything to twist the tail of the British Lion, it is as good as done. What else do you think I have been working for? I have concentrated on crime for years, I have developed a reputation carefully, I planned it so that there is no single loophole. I worked it so that you thought I was interested only in blackmail, and I took those women to make you think it was even more abnormal, a man who had lost his mind. *That* is what you thought, you and Chatsworth.'

Roger said nothing, but watched tensely. There was no point in interrupting, he could not make this man say anything that he wanted to keep to himself.

'Only recently have you realised there might be something bigger in it,' said Riordon. 'Well, there is! I made this village, I financed the builder who put up all the new houses, I bought this inn and put my own landlord in, I have held the women and the men here, *all* at the instigation of Moscow. Do you understand?'

'Yes. Go on,' Roger said very slowly.

'I had helpers, West. I did not think much of them at the time, but they were able to tell me what men to take, what keymen would do the nuclear effort most harm if they were taken away.' He paused and an incredibly cunning gleam entered his eyes. 'At the Home Office, the Service Ministries, and the BBC, I thought I had been betrayed by one of them, but I found I had not. Amy Groves and Banks and Allen all did their best, they took their money and told me what was necessary, but the time came when they had to be killed. And my colleagues? They will go on even with me dead. Even when dead I shall go on turning my sword in England's heart. You can try for a year, for a lifetime, but you will never find *them*. They have outsmarted you, and if they used me to do it what do I care? Let me tell you something else. They were coming here to see me. The map was prepared for them, but I thought someone had stolen it. I didn't know you had it. And they didn't come. They are safe. They go scot-free with the biggest prize – access to all Britain's secrets. I do not care a single damn for anything else. I know who they are, West, and I can name them. No one else can. Just me, you understand?'

He paused, and his voice fell very low.

'Do you think I will talk? Do you think you can make me even if I lived? But do you think I want to live, now. You have more than one murder proved against me. I killed Parker and Sloan, and the dwarf Richardson, and you can prove it. The weapon's here, with my prints on, and I am wounded so that I cannot get away. The thing I threw at you, killed them, and it has Richardson's blood on it, too. But you will not hang me or shoot me, you will not try to make me talk, because I am going to kill myself. While I was free, while I had a chance, I wanted to live and to go on fighting you, but I am better out of the way, now. They call it *hara-kiri* in Japan. Perhaps you have a better word for it. Watch!'

Roger jumped to his feet. At the same moment a man came out of the back door, windows went up and men started to climb through. Riordon flung his head back and bellowed with laughter as they rushed towards him.

Before they reached him he put a gun to his open mouth.

'Not a Bad Idea,' Says Chatsworth

THE LAST LAUGH was cut short, even before the roar of the shot.

Roger was nearest the man, and saw exactly what happened. He drew up short, then turned away as Riordon fell back.

Riordon was dead, but had never created greater horror than in the moment of his dying.

It was some time afterwards when night had fallen and lights were on in the little lounge of *The Trout and the Fly,* that Chatsworth, Roger, Pep Morgan, Marion and two police superintendents had gathered. Before then Morgan had explained a little, but the story had little effect on Roger, whose concern was for the missing men and who cared little that he had been deceived by Chatsworth and Morgan as well as Riordon.

In some ways it was simple.

Chatsworth had outmatched Riordon in cunning in one way at least. He had nursed the idea that Roger was the focal point of the investigation, had stressed his dependence on him – and had worked with others, including Morgan. Riordon's attention had been diverted to Roger, while Morgan and Chatsworth and others had gone at high pressure. Roger had not even been told of the discovery, some days before, that Riordon 'owned' Woodhill – inquiries which Chatsworth had set in motion after the first mention of the village had proved that.

'So he had two men sent down here – you thought it was on your suggestion, Handsome, but he wanted them to fox

Riordon. Chatsworth's got a mind nearly as bad as that man had.' Morgan had smiled as he said that. 'Then I came down with some others, and we kept our eyes open. We managed to catch a glimpse of Riordon once or twice. He let Marion Byrne stay down here because he thought we'd think he wouldn't be such a fool as to allow her to stay at the very place where he was working. It nearly came off, but not quite – he let himself be spotted, you see. And then I was near Hinton this morning and I saw Riordon heading away on his motorbike. I was able to follow him. I saw him kill that poor little dwarf,' Morgan had added with a twist to his lips. 'He *was* mad.'

'Three parts, anyhow,' Roger had admitted slowly.

'Four parts, in my opinion,' Morgan had said. 'Well we expected he would expect you, and guessed he had plenty waiting for you. But he *didn't* know that we'd got at the innkeeper, who had worked for him for a long time. Proper old lag, but that didn't matter. We got at him, told him we wouldn't proceed with any charges if he helped us. He hid me in the place, and Chatsworth and the military were not far away – the military were on ordinary manoeuvres, nothing surprising in that. We knew he'd concentrate on you. He had men in those houses, the way he said, and the thing they didn't know was that the military were coming in to attack, and had put a cordon round the village. You following me?'

Roger had nodded.

'We had to let things go on for a bit,' Morgan had continued, 'we had to wait until the military were all ready. Remember that explosion? That was the signal, we knew we could get going then. You threw that tear gas and it helped all right, but I released some more upstairs. It smoked Riordon out. He was alone in the pub, you see, except for the innkeeper – or he thought he was. He thought you were the only one with tear-gas, and that he would be all right when he got outside. But his men didn't start shooting properly because they weren't given time. There wasn't much trouble.' Morgan drew a deep breath, then smiled somewhat apologetically. 'I hope you don't feel too bad about it, Handsome. I had to do what the Assistant Commissioner told me.'

Roger had wrinkled his brow. 'My feelings don't matter, and they're not particularly sore. We wanted results and you got them. But we still haven't got the men who matter.'

Morgan had rubbed his chin, as if gloomily.

When Chatsworth and the others came in it was clear that he was feeling glum, although he said little about it. There was a sense of anticlimax which Roger found maddening. It was not relieved by the news that Mark, not badly hurt, was already in Newbury Hospital. There were men as dangerous as Riordon, perhaps more dangerous because they were not known. And they still had the prisoners, there was no indication of the whereabouts of the prison itself.

Chatsworth showed his feelings with an explosive: 'For all we know they might be dead. Hasn't anyone got a worthwhile idea?' He glared about him, then shrugged. 'Well, we'll have to get going. Nothing else to do. But we start off worse than we were before, and—'

'Just a moment,' said Roger.

Chatsworth paused, and the others stared at Roger, who was frowning as he contemplated his Chief. An idea, no more than the germ so far, had entered his mind. Expert in the laying of false trails, Riordon had maintained that practice throughout. His method had been one gigantic bluff. Was there any reason to suppose that he had changed in the last few minutes of his life?

'Well, what is it?' demanded Chatsworth.

Roger said slowly: 'Is there any news about that bus driver?'

'Bus driver!' snorted Chatsworth. 'Now what's getting into you, West?'

'The bus driver,' repeated Roger firmly. 'Who gave him that trunk?'

'The proprietor here,' answered Chatsworth. 'That was why Riordon had the fellow killed. He was killed, no question of that of course. But if you'll be good enough, West, to give me an idea of what you are driving at, I shall be grateful.'

Roger said: 'The bus driver was an innocent victim?'

'Well?'

'Amy Groves, Allen and Banks were thought to be innocent victims,' continued Roger very softly. 'Riordon told us that they worked for him, but that he killed them when their job was finished. It could be a part of the bluff. Riordon really went overboard on the matter of that map. Someone had betrayed him, he said, by losing or giving away a map. That map, and copies of it, were needed by his colleagues due to come here for the first time. It gave nothing away unless one had the key, when it gave everything away. And Riordon thought someone had stolen a copy. He was right – Richardson had. But that doesn't matter. The fact that these men who worked with him are still alive, does matter.'

Chatsworth urged: 'Well, go on, West.'

'There is no hurry,' said Roger. 'They will be waiting for us when we get to London. Riordon once tried to make out that the clerks were his agents, but supposing those clerks were innocent victims like the bus driver? And for the same reason: they could name his associates. Supposing Riordon knew that their story could betray the men he wanted to protect and to distract our attention from: the men he *did go to* visit.' Roger paused, and then added: 'I mean, Commander Morris, Sir William Bennett and Mr Michison. Well, sir?'

'Not a bad idea,' conceded Chatsworth, after a long pause. 'Not a bad idea at all. But why are we sitting here doing nothing?'

Before they left Woodhill Chatsworth telephoned the Yard to give instructions for the three men to be shadowed even more closely. And on Roger's suggestion a telephone call was to be sent to them, telling them to go to Michison's flat at eleven o'clock the next morning. Chatsworth told Roger on the way to London, in the early hours of the morning, that the three had behaved normally enough since Roger had interviewed them.

Cartwright had returned to Dorchester. Marion was staying in a Newbury hotel because she thought Mark would like to feel that someone was showing interest in him. Woodhill was still in the hands of the police, while from Newbury telegrams were despatched to numerous anxious relatives.

It was odd, Roger thought, as he sat next to Chatsworth, with Pep Morgan in the back of the AC's large limousine, that he had seen little of the women who had played so large a part in Riordon's great bluff. But he had discovered that they were, without exception, addicted to drugs. Some more than others, it had been found, and most of them stayed at Woodhill, believing that while there they had a chance of recovery. Riordon had even gone so far as to employ a qualified doctor, who had 'treated' them.

Later, Roger was to discover much more of the precautions which Riordon had taken, to learn that the two or three women who had been released had been subjected to a course of 'horror treatment' which, added to the drugs, had reduced them to a state of physical and mental prostration. Amongst other discoveries in the village of Woodhill were many reels of Korean war horror films, many of them far worse than Roger had imagined to be in existence. The effect of them on the highly strung, drug-stimulated victims had been great; there were times when he considered the ruthlessness of Riordon with a sense of dread that left him in a cold sweat. The influence of Riordon did not leave him for a long time afterwards; there were times when he dreamed of the man, and woke up in a frenzy.

Through that trying period Janet had sustained him more than anyone else.

He had little knowledge of these things, and no idea how it would work out, as he sat next to Chatsworth and sped towards London through the darkness. Two police cars followed. The body of Riordon would be brought back by ambulance. The Newbury police, with some Yard men, were going through the village systematically, and doctors and nurses had been summoned from Newbury to help Riordon's women victims.

Roger thought little about that: he was thinking most of Michison and trying to work the thing out. If he were right the explosive radiogram had been just another incident in a chain of many to confuse him. He had wondered all along why that comparatively innocuous infernal machine had been used. Moreover if Michison were involved then Riordon's use of his flat was explained.

He thought far less of the blustering Bennett and the dapper Morris: Michison had impressed himself on his mind more than either of the others. There was 'Fluff', too.

At times during that journey he told himself that the idea had been no more than a wild guess, that it was hopelessly wide of the mark. Yet it persisted, and on the way he made all the necessary arrangements.

From the Yard, reached as dawn broke, he went first to Fulham. He found that his cabin trunk was missing, of course, and discovered that the police guard had been taken off after Mark had left for Hinton Magna; a burglary had been reported the next day.

Certainly Riordon had done nothing by halves.

Then Roger went to Michison's flat.

The area was cordoned off by police and there was no way in which Michison and his wife could get away. If they tried to, it would mean that they had succeeded in getting past him and that would not be too good for him. He went alone, straight from Fulham, because of the possibility that he was being followed. He wanted to create the impression that it was a friendly call.

It was gloomy inside the house, and the stairs creaked as he went up. He had a momentary feeling of alarm lest the tenants had gone, but when he knocked on the door there was a sound of movement inside and a moment later Fluff opened the door.

She stared at him for a moment, and then widened her eyes.

'Why, hallo, policeman,' she said, and stood aside for him to enter.

'Hallo, Mrs Michison,' said Roger cheerfully. 'Is your husband in?'

'He's getting ready to go to the office,' declared Fluff, 'and I'm just making some coffee. Will you have a cup?'

'I'd like one very much,' said Roger.

The lounge was not being used, but some easy chairs had been taken into the dining room, where he was left for a few minutes smoking a cigarette. Then Michison came in, straightening his tie; there was a slight cut on his chin, from shaving. His smile was ready and infectious, and a wave of depression attacked Roger.

He forced it back, however, and said easily: 'I thought you'd like to know that your worries are over.'

'Worries?' Michison raised his eyebrows. 'I didn't know that I had any. Oh, of course – police suspicion! And the attentions of Count Riordon, too. Don't tell me you've caught the ungallant Count?'

Was there a touch of overeagerness in the question?

Fluff brought in coffee.

'Caught whom?' she asked as she poured it out.

'The great Count Riordon,' said Michison. 'How's the poor chap that was hurt – I've forgotten his name. One of your sergeants, wasn't he?'

'He's on the mend,' said Roger, 'but he hasn't been able to make a report yet. However, with Riordon in the bag there's no need to worry.' He looked very content as he sat back in an easy chair and sipped his coffee, trying to judge the moment to spring his bombshell. *If* they were implicated, he would know when he sprung the trap: if they weren't he would look many kinds of a fool. Metaphorically he shrugged his shoulders.

'He was a nasty customer, wasn't he?' said Michison. 'What was his particular game? Or shouldn't I inquire?' He looked ingenuously into Roger's eyes.

'There's no harm in inquiring,' said Roger. 'But why take the trouble? He talked. He thought he could hold out, but he couldn't. Bennett and Morris are under arrest, and—'

The reaction came swiftly. One moment Michison had been lounging back nonchalantly. The next his hand dropped to his pocket; the trap had been sprung. The woman flung her coffee at Roger's face. It missed, although some splashed him. Roger slid down into his chair and kicked upwards at Michison's hand, in which a gun appeared. The gun was pushed upwards although he kept his grip on it. His face had hardened, his wife's was hard with desperation. Neither of them spoke, and Fluff flung another cup at Roger: hot liquid spilled over his forehead but did not stop him from taking a familiar tube of tear gas from his breast pocket. As he tossed it towards the others, and ducked again, he heard a sound at the door. Michison staggered back, and Fluff turned towards the door.

'What—' a man said in alarm.

As the gas began to take effect again, Roger saw and recognised dapper Commander Morris, and knew that the telephone trick had worked. Bennett would soon be here, and Yard men would follow them both. Whatever happened to him the case was over. As the others staggered about with tears streaming from their eyes he backed to a corner of the room. Morris stood on the threshold, then turned abruptly. He cannoned into Bennett, who was on the threshold, and, through a haze, Roger saw the Yard men crowding the landing behind Morris.

Then he let discretion be the better part of valour and ducked behind one of the easy chairs.

Bennett and Morris walked straight into the trap, and the Michison's reaction had been so prompt that Roger knew the strain at which they had been living. He knew little about what followed at the flat except that the Yard men had gas masks; actually the struggle had been short-lived.

He was not surprised that Bennett was the first to break

down and to give the news for which all of them had been waiting: the missing men were alive. Roger felt very rueful about the place where they were imprisoned: they were in the cellar of the house which Michison owned, and where he had occupied the top floor flat. They had not been ill-treated, but had been told that they would not leave the cellar alive unless they put the results of their investigations on paper. But no great efforts had been made to persuade them, Roger discovered: Riordon and the others had waited for the passing of the storm, dealing with the first danger first.

Later in the day, in Chatsworth's office, the AC said: 'It certainly wasn't a bad idea, West. Mind you, we wouldn't have left them alone, but they might have done a great deal more harm before we caught them. The credit's yours.' Chatsworth was at his most amiable. 'We all have to have a slice or two of luck sometimes, don't we?'

'Luck?' asked Roger.

'Now, come, it was just a chance thought,' said Chatsworth. 'Own up.'

Roger put his head on one side. 'I was lucky that I was hauled out of the river, I was lucky at *The Trout and the Fly,* and it was touch and go whether I came out of the Michisons' flat alive. But be fair, sir! I followed Riordon's methods of fighting us, and they could only lead to Michison and company.' He paused for a moment, then added slyly: 'I can't understand why no one else thought of it.'

'That's enough from you,' said Chatsworth, and chuckled. 'I won't deny it, though, it was there for all of us to see. Seriously, what do you consider the turning point in the affair? My hoodwinking you and letting you take the first fire?'

'That, yes,' said Roger ruefully. 'And little Richardson, of course. It was queer, sir, that dwarf should have no social conscience at all but be so intensely patriotic.' He paused as Chatsworth nodded and then added: 'Is there anything else?'

'No, not now,' said Chatsworth. 'The *Concerto* problem was easy, after all. Records, the dwarf – who so often gave warning

– and the BBC artiste, as another red herring. All the same, it did give an uncanny touch. Well, I'd like a full report as soon as you can prepare it but there's no real hurry. We've got our men, both ours and Riordon's. And the pressure from above is no longer worrying. Thanks, West.'

Roger smiled, and said 'thank you', and then walked from Westminster to Fulham. From Bell Street he telephoned Janet, and was implored to have a word with Paula, who wanted to know how Mark and Marion were.

'Mark's in a pretty helpless state in hospital,' said Roger. 'Marion ought to find it easy.'

'You pig!' exclaimed Paula, and he heard her add: 'Isn't he, Jan? Oh, of course, you *wouldn't* think so.' She said goodbye, laughingly. Then Janet came to the phone again to say that she would catch an early train in the morning, but would he try to get a few pieces of fish for Quiz. And: 'Go to bed early, darling, you must get plenty of sleep.'

'Not a bad idea,' said Roger. 'Tomorrow then, my sweet.'

And he rang off.

JOHN CREASEY

GIDEON'S DAY

Gideon's day is a busy one. He balances family commitments with solving a series of seemingly unrelated crimes from which a plot nonetheless evolves and a mystery is solved.

One of the most senior officers within Scotland Yard, George Gideon's crime solving abilities are in the finest traditions of London's world famous police headquarters. His analytical brain and sense of fairness is respected by colleagues and villains alike.

'The finest of all Scotland Yard series' – New York Times.

GIDEON'S FIRE

Commander George Gideon of Scotland Yard has to deal successively with news of a mass murderer, a depraved maniac, and the deaths of a family in an arson attack on an old building south of the river. This leaves little time for the crisis developing at home ....

'Gideon of Scotland Yard emerges as one of the most real working detectives in modern fiction.... A sympathetic and believable professional policeman.' - New York Times

JOHN CREASEY

INSPECTOR WEST TAKES CHARGE

Extortion is the name of the game and the method includes murdering anyone who might get in the way. Who will control the Dreem factory and much else is at stake.

Inspector West has to unravel it all at gun point, but not without difficulty and surprise . . .

The Case Against Paul Raeburn

Chief Inspector Roger West has been watching and waiting for over two years – he is determined to catch Paul Raeburn out. The millionaire racketeer may have made a mistake, following the killing of a small time crook.

Can the ace detective triumph over the evil Raeburn in what are very difficult circumstances? This cannot be assumed as not eveything, it would seem, is as simple as it first appears .....

INTRODUCING THE TOFF

Whilst returning home from a cricket match at his father's country home, the Honourable Richard Rollison - alias The Toff - comes across an accident which proves to be a mystery. As he delves deeper into the matter with his usual perseverance and thoroughness , murder and suspense form the backdrop to a fast moving and exciting adventure.

'The Toff has been promoted to a place of honour among amateur detectives.' – The Times Literary Supplement

JOHN CREASEY

THE HOUSE OF THE BEARS

Standing alone in the bleak Yorkshire Moors is Sir Rufus Marne's 'House of the Bears'. Dr. Palfrey is asked to journey there to examine an invalid - who has now disappeared. Moreover, Marne's daughter lies terribly injured after a fall from the minstrel's gallery which Dr. Palfrey discovers was no accident. He sets out to investigate and the results surprise even him . . . .

"'Palfrey' and his boys deserve to take their places among the immortals." - Western Mail